INTERSTELLAR FLIGHT MAGAZINE

Best of Year Two

Interstellar Flight Press

INTERSTELLAR FLIGHT PRESS BEST OF YEAR TWO

Cover Illustration by Suk Hyun Jung.

Edited by Holly Lyn Walrath and Sydney Richardson.

Published by Interstellar Flight Press, Houston, Texas.

www.interstellarflightpress.com

ISBN (eBook): 978-1-953736-06-2

ISBN (paperback): 978-1-953736-07-9

First Edition: August 2021

Edited by

Holly Lyn Walrath
Sydney Richardson
Jamileh Jemison

Contributors

Leslie Archibald
Erin Becker
Cassandra Rose Clarke
Laura Díaz de Arce
Nathan Elias
Michael Glazner
Allison Hunt
Nisola Jegede
Justin Key
Annika Barranti Klein
Andrea Kriz
vanessa maki
Natachi Mez
Archita Mittra
JT Morse
B Narr
Karen A. Romanko
Christina Sng
Bonnie Jo Stufflebeam
Suhaila Sundararajan
Kyle Tam
Presley Thomas
Tlotlo Tsamaase
John Tuttle
T.D. Walker
Corey J. White

Featuring Interviews with

Martha Wells
Tochi Onyebuchi
Jessica Guess
Laura Lam
Julia Ember
Sarah Gailey
Cassandra Rose Clarke
Catherine Moore
Andrea Blythe

Contents

Reviews

Interviews

2020 Alternate Endings

Editor's Note

BY HOLLY LYN WALRATH

It's strange to look back on the last year from 2021, which feels so far removed from a year ago. 2020 was a year of contradictions. Sequestered at home, many of the writers I know suddenly had enough time to complete that project waiting for their attention. But as a whole, we struggled to finish anything worthwhile. Between the cycling news presenting a daily blogroll of trauma, violence, and despair, and the very-real impacts of a global pandemic, it was a rough year, to say the least.

A vast myriad of darkness faced us in 2020. From Australian bushfires to the COVID-19 pandemic, the impeachment of the U.S. President to the stock market crash, the Black Lives Matter protests to wildfires in the U.S., the death of Chadwick Boseman (Rest in Power, King) to the death of Supreme Court Justice Ruth Bader Ginsburg. It's difficult to process everything that happened. There was a sense of surreality about the year, as if, like Erin Becker's dark and humorous essay, "Your Critique Group's Feedback on Covid-19" the year 2020 had been written by a fledgling science fiction writer with a zeal for the bizarre.

For myself, it was a year of personal tragedy and illness. Working with the huge crew of volunteers and writers at Interstellar Flight Press kept me inspired, engaged, and humble. When I read the stories and articles in this anthology, I'm reminded that the world does have some light amongst the grim darkness. This anthology covers a wide range of topics and media, from books to anime to film to television to feminism to queerness to racism and beyond. Our authors dove into complex and often heated discussion topics with nuance, expressing the idea that although 2020 may have broken us, it hasn't beaten us.

Our biggest achievement this year, in my humble opinion as editor, was our 2020 alternate endings short story call, edited by Jamileh Jemison. I was hesitant to open this call because I worried: Is it asking too much to ask writers to dwell in the bleakness of 2020? I know how difficult it can be to be asked to write about trauma. But Jamileh helmed our little starship with grace, picking stories that represent the wide galaxy of 2020. The stories we received surprised me and pushed me to see that although 2020 was one big dumpster fire, that doesn't have to be the ending we choose.

As Jamileh says, "Want a better world? Get as many people dreaming one up as possible! The stories we tell give those dreams voice, and when we all raise our voices, we drive change."

I owe a debt of gratitude to my co-editor, Sydney Richardson, a fantastic writer in her own right, for helping me keep track of submissions, send contracts to writers, and make sure articles get published on time. Thank you to our contributors and volunteers for this amazing anthology. Every year, you astound me.

Original Articles

Escapism as a Way of Coping: Diving into
New Realms of Fantasy to Process Emotions

BY ALLISON HUNT

Harry Potter spoilers ahead!

More so now than ever before, with everything that's going on in the world, I have needed to submerge myself into a new realm.

Whether I was attempting to make a pencil move with just my eyes as a six-year-old after watching *Matilda,* or yelling at my dad as an eight-year-old in the car to make it home in time to catch Melissa Joan Hart in *Sabrina the Teenage Witch* on ABC's programming block TGIF (true story btw), I have always had an affinity for magic and witches.

Harry Potter and the Sorcerer's Stone was the first fantasy novel I ever remember reading (basic I know, but like come on, I don't think you'd be reading this article if you weren't a Potterhead). I picked up the novel for the first time when I was nine after my older sister read it and, like almost all of us, couldn't get through the first four chapters. However, upon starting it again at the age of eleven, I was officially hooked.

I had never been more entranced in a story before and I couldn't get enough. I inhaled the first five books. I even remember my mom getting mad at me for staying up until four in the morning reading, but I literally couldn't put them down. Having to wait a couple of years for the next book was truly torture.

But that torture was nothing compared to my dad passing away in March of 2005. I don't want to go into this too much, but it really sucked and still sucks. Just a couple months later in July, *Harry Potter and the Half-Blood Prince* was set to come out. Masking my need to escape from my reality by re-reading the first five books in order to prepare for the 6th installment was truly a blessing. Never had I ever wanted to change my present circumstances more. I remember finding solace in the *Wizarding World of Harry Potter*: it was where I would go to get away from it all when I needed it the most.

Well, as you know, or should know at this point if you're a die-hard Potterhead, at the end of Half-blood prince, Harry's mentor, Albus Dumbledore, dies. I could've thought of this as some sort of sick joke that the universe was playing on me but honestly, reading about Harry's grief helped me to process mine. I had never been able to relate to a character more—and being able to not only sympathize but empathize with Harry and the pain he was feeling was very cathartic and healing for me.

From that point on, anytime I was going through something difficult in my personal life, no matter how big or small, I would pick up a fantasy or dystopian novel and dive into a new world. When I was having a hard time freshman year of college and truly unhappy where I was at, Katniss Everdeen's trials and tribulations made mine seem frivolous at best. Upon transferring schools and still feeling lonely and out of place, Tris Prior from *The Divergent Series* by Veronica Roth (*Katherine Tegen Books,* 2016) and the post-apocalyptic society in which she lives was there to take me out of my head and into hers.

Even as an adult, when I was in a toxic relationship, I discovered the *Throne of Glass* series by Sarah J. Maas (*Bloomsbury USA Childrens,* 2012). Immersing myself into the Kingdom of Adarlan and Celaena Sardothien's epic adventure and emotional struggles enabled me to not only break free from my current reality but also to work through it. I realize now, in retrospect, that all the series I mentioned above are young adult books. I personally feel that these novels capture the emotional turmoil and growth of their characters in a deeper way, and therefore always put me in my feelings more than adult fantasy/dystopian novels do.

I'm really not trying to sound like "woe is me." These moments in time are just that—moments— from my overall joyful and fulfilling life. Being able to so thoroughly immerse myself into these epic worlds and stories made the times when I would put the book down and come back to my own present circumstances seem not so bad.

More so now than ever before, with everything that's going on in the world, I have needed to submerge myself into a new realm. At the beginning of quarantine, I finally had time to pick up *The Queen of Tearling* series by Erika Johansen (*Harper*, 2014) that had been collecting dust on my shelf. It was just what the "doctor" ordered to calm my anxiety and worry.

Dystopian and fantasy novels are my form of therapy, so to speak; my personal form of escapism, and a way for me to relate and process difficult emotions.

To be clear, I think mental health and healthy coping mechanisms are so important. I am not by any means saying that reading *Lord of the Rings* should replace seeing a licensed professional. I feel that everyone, myself included, could benefit from therapy.

That being said, reading is definitely one of my favorite forms of self-care: crawling up on the couch on a rainy day with a cup of coffee in one hand, and a good novel in the other, is my happy place. It has now been a couple of months since I finished my last fantasy novel, and I am definitely due for another session.

NOTE FROM THE AUTHOR: I grew up loving the Harry Potter series. I have read all 7 books more times than I can count. And as explained through this article, the book helped me process my own personal grief. I also identify as an LGBTQ+ ally so I would be remiss if I did not comment on J.K. Rowling's harmful behavior. I honestly have been having a hard time processing my experience and love of the books, with the actions of its author. Harry Potter is a book of magic and love and wonder and hope and I am trying to hold onto those themes. Trans women are women. Trans men are men.

Your Critique Group's Feedback on Covid-19: Thanks for sharing this really interesting story!

BY ERIN BECKER

We're partial to your typical contemporary realistic pieces, if we're honest. But we understand these forays into speculative fiction—like that dystopia kick back in 2016—have proven a fruitful source of experimentation.

We do, however, have some questions.

First. What genre *is* this, exactly? The whole mutated-virus storyline is squarely sci-fi. And the nonchalant, brazenly market-focused government response—if a little on-the-nose—felt appropriate to the "bleak yet believable near-future" aesthetic you seem to be going for.

But given the epic stakes, it's odd that the characters primarily respond by looking up best practices for sourdough starter and revisiting old arguments about *Avatar: The Last Airbender* ships.

Sorry, what? We get you're trying to make these folks relatable. But no reader wants to imagine they'll spend the end times squabbling over how loudly one is permitted to type while sharing a home office. Or whether soaking a Pyrex in soapy water is an intentional abdication of dishwashing duties.

Is this one of those "commentary on modern society" things? If so, we're totally missing it. Maybe rethink your strategy.

Speaking of activity in the end times. (Sexual activity, specifically.) We anticipated this story would be romantic and even erotically charged, given the close quarters and backdrop of deep unpredictability. You know the tropes: snowed in at the cabin. There's only one bed. Arranged marriage, even. Your characters are *literally* trapped in a house together. It's a love story goldmine!

Given all that, we're not really sure where you're going with this routine where they keep falling into bed together after getting wine-drunk on Zoom, then mutually deciding they'll do it tomorrow.

This seems like an intentional undermining of the audience's expectations. And not in a good way. Consider revisiting.

Also. Let's talk about foreshadowing. There were a few warnings early in the text that an event like this could happen. But the virus introduced at the end of the first act really has no thematic resonance with what was established in the opening.

It's just so...random?

Sure, the pandemic jars the protagonists out of their deeply troubling complacency. But does it jar them in a way that is at all relevant to their character arcs?

We'll have to see what you do with the climax. But we're not really sure this plot makes any sense.

Finally, the key issue with this draft. So, the protagonists' goal is to beat the virus. And that's fine—if, again, a bit random, given where we thought this story was going. But as readers, we're hoping to see these characters actually *do* stuff. And you haven't given your protagonists any tools for taking action against this large-scale threat.

Okay, there's that scene where they post some "isolation selfies" on their Instagram. And another where they bravely toss boxes of organic cereal into a supermarket cart while wearing a face mask from that cute Etsy shop.

Still, it doesn't really feel like enough.

Could we get a battle on a rocketship or something? A few badass lasers?

Protective gear with more swagger than flannel pajama bottoms, at least?

Consider you might have created parameters that make it impossible for your characters to establish themselves as plausible heroes of this story.

Don't worry, though. It's just a first draft. We're confident you'll figure it out in revision.

The Pixel Campfire: Indie Horror in the Age of the Internet: How Marginalized Creators are Reshaping Horror

BY B. NARR

"The internet has given marginalized creators a platform to tell their stories exactly how they want and to tell stories that have needed to be told for years."

We've always told scary stories around the campfire, trying to explain what lurks beyond the safety of its light, trying to lend shape to the unknown. Horror is an integral part of the human experience. Consuming horror in media is a safe, communal way to explore our fears—it assures us we're not alone and that, no matter how bad things are, we can make it out alive. That's something we all deserve to take part in.

Until recently, though, the genre (like many others) has been constrained by the gatekeepers of traditional media. The metaphorical "campfire" was the movie industry, the radio industry, the publishing industry—mediums controlled by a small group of privileged people. A lot of folks weren't allowed to tell their stories. Now, the world of creative work is rapidly changing, all because of one thing.

We have the internet: the largest campfire in human history.

With virtually no barrier between creator and consumer, diverse media can flourish. Not only can people tell their stories unhindered, but consumers can say *yes, I want more of that* and actually be heard. Nowhere is this more obvious than in the indie horror community. From webcomics and podcasts to anthologies and animated shows, to more experimental mediums like microfiction and minicomics, marginalized creators are leading horror into a wonderful new age, backed by fans who truly believe in their work.

Malaise: A Horror Anthology (Jessamine Press, 2018) is a prime example of what can be done in this new system. It's an anthology written solely by POC, LGBTQ+, and disabled authors that was crowdfunded on Kickstarter, and is now available through Gumroad. It was put together for the sole purpose of telling stories "written by voices often unheard in the publishing world." That's exactly what indie horror is all about—highlighting stories that otherwise wouldn't get heard and creating ones that speak your truth.

Tonia Thompson, the founder of *Nightlight Pod,* is doing just that. Nightlight Pod is an ongoing audio anthology written by black horror authors and narrated by black actors. Occasionally she writes for it, but it's largely composed of submitted short stories from other black horror writers all around the world. This collaborative aspect of new indie horror makes it exceptionally powerful. You can build teams that, otherwise, wouldn't ever have met.

You can also build teams that, pre-internet, would only exist in a professional studio. The folks behind *Teething* are a team like that. Son M., an Arab horror writer, and Jess Lackey, a sapphic character and creature designer, are creating an entire LGBTQ+/horror/dark comedy animated show together. Being able to gather animators and build hype online, not to mention crowdfunding it in the future, is what makes this massive project possible for indie creators.

The internet has given also given people the resources to create amazing things by themselves that would, traditionally, require backing from a large publisher, as Filipina author and illustrator Alexa Sharpe proves with her haunting book *Dressed for Death* (2018). She wrote, illustrated, and published the entire anthology herself.

Solo creators have branched out to more internet-dependent mediums, as well. *Carnival de Cuentos* is a testament to the endless possibilities that come with embracing this. Knightie, a nonbinary Mexican-American writer and illustrator, has created this "spooky magical series" that could pretty much only exist online. There's a website that explains the whole universe in-depth, character art on said website and all over their social media, and the first story in the series is available serial-style on AO3. Their range is amazing. The medium freely morphs with what the story needs, rather than vice versa.

That phenomenon has birthed a few different mediums, like the minicomic. Unlike traditional comic strips, these comics can be pretty much any length (despite *mini* being in the name), any format, and about literally anything–including subject matter too visceral for any other outlet. Take *They Were Normal People,* created by Spanish artist Dood (2019), for instance. It's a minicomic about anti-queer violence and the banality of evil. (Content warning for, well... All of that.) It's a gut-punch of a story—and one that most of us wouldn't get to see without the internet.

That's the part of indie horror that is, in my opinion, the most important. The internet has given marginalized creators a platform to tell their stories exactly how they want and to tell stories that have needed to be told for years. Not only are they now able to do so in revolutionary new mediums, but they can publicly take part in a genre that's integral to exploring the fears of our era—a genre that inherently needs to be diverse to be universally truthful.

Final Girl: A Life in Horror: The Making of a Horror Writer

BY CHRISTINA SNG

Editor's Note: This essay was a finalist for the Bram Stoker Award Superior Achievement in Short Non-Fiction.

For as long as I can remember, I've always been a child of horror. Every night, after my mother read to me and tucked me in, I kept my hands and feet safely under my blanket to make sure the monsters under my bed didn't eat them. Even at that young age, I knew our limbs didn't regenerate.

This was the 70s, when horror blew our minds with films like The Amityville Horror (1977) and Dawn of the Dead (1978). My older brother and I were huge horror movie fans, and it seemed back then every other week there was something new on TV.

During the scary parts, he always laughed, which diluted the fear factor for me, and soon, I began to laugh too. I mean, who wanted to look like a scaredy-cat next to their big brother? Pretty soon, I was no longer scared.

Outside the home—my safe space—I was bullied through my childhood years despite occasional kindnesses from unexpected places. I survived the rest of grade school by being aloof and acting tough and made it out in one piece. There were no horror role models who were my age then, not until I reached my teens and met Nancy Thomson and Marti Gaines.

The 80s ushered me into my teen years with the Poltergeist trilogy, the Nightmare on Elm Street series, and *Hell Night* (1981), which really stayed with me because of that closing scene—the final girl surviving all the monsters with only her wits and instincts.

I thought if she could survive that, surely I could survive life. And here's the thing, women in horror movies are tough.

In *Poltergeist*, Diane Freeling enters another dimension and swims through a pool full of rotting corpses to save her children. Nancy Thomson faces her fears and defeats the serial killer Freddy Krueger in *A Nightmare on Elm Street*. And in *Hell Night*, Marti Gaines' clear thinking and decisive actions save her from being another victim of the Garth brothers. For Marti, hell really is other people.

In contrast, I was far from tough. In high school, I realized I still had no clue how to make friends, ending up ostracized in whisper campaigns and surrounded by uneasy alliances instead. It was a whole other jungle. Horror films seemed to exist in a much simpler world where the final girl always won.

So I got myself tougher and took up martial arts. Soon, I exuded new confidence. I could handle myself in any situation. Things didn't get easier at school but I no longer cared what others thought. I was no longer scared of anything.

Of course, life in horror movies was far worse than mine. That gave me a measure of comfort and solace. No matter how bad things got, it never got to the point where I'd be hunted by a killer at home or had my dreams invaded by monsters. (Not yet, anyway. I mean, I'm writing this in 2020 and this year's motto seems to be *Anything is Possible*.)

Then somehow, slowly, in school and in church, I began to make my first friends and found my place in both worlds.

I loved my youth group and joined the church choir despite sounding like a strangled canary prodded by a taser. I even read for mass, uncovering a flair for elocution.

In school, I discovered that I was particularly good at sports and writing. I ran long distance, dabbled in swimming, and took up Judo and Karate, and began writing fiction and poetry.

Writing was cathartic for me in a world where no one understood me.

Emotions were too difficult for me to process as a teenager and I felt lighter after pouring my heart out on paper and truly, that saved me innumerable times from the albatross of depression.

The genre I wrote in was, of course, horror. It was the genre I grew up with, in a house of shadows that gave me safety and comfort, the genre I had happy memories with and was still deeply immersed in as the media's love affair with horror raged on.

Yet it was always horror novels and British girls' magazines that brought me the greatest joy.

After church every Sunday, I'd race down to the market where I would grab the latest issue of *Misty*, *Girl*, *Princess*, and *Tammy* by UK's Fleetway Publications, all of which featured mystery and horror comics for girls at the newsstand.

Fantastically written, drawn, and with enough supernatural and mystical elements to intrigue a young reader, the stories were always about girls, (both the heroes and the villains), and they truly resonated with me.

I treasured my collection. Yet the entirety of it was lost when one day, my mother threw my neatly packed box of comics away. I have spent most of my adult working life looking for all my favorite issues, and to my relief, I've recovered a good many of them to share with my children who love and cherish them as much as I do.

At the same time, I began reading voraciously and devoured a plethora of horror novels from authors like Robert McCammon and Dean Koontz, as well as both the horror book series for teens, Dark Forces and the Dell Twilight Series: Where Darkness Begins, that I collected from local used bookstores, prolific during that era, bringing in books I could never find in regular bookstores.

The Dell Twilight Series: Where Darkness Begins featured several of my still-favorite books, preciously guarded out-of-print volumes, *Watery*

Grave by Joseph Trainor (1983), *Demon Tree* by Colin Daniels (1983), *Voices in the Dark* by James Haynes (1982), and *Storm Child* by Susan Netter (1983), reminiscent of Christopher Pike's later series of books. They are still some of the coolest stories I've ever read and the books stay close to me on my bedside book trolley.

I wrote fiction throughout my teen years. One of the things I enjoyed most was writing horror novelettes in longhand during class and passing the small hardcover books to classmates who were keen to read them. When they were done, they'd ask me to quickly write the next installment.

It was the first validation I had that my writing had value and an audience. The stories were about teens with telekinesis struggling with issues we all faced. It was an instant hit and soon, I became more than just the Mentos dealer in class. I became a novelist.

Over the decades, horror has helped me shut down overwhelming emotions. Watching *Buffy* and *Angel* gave me comfort, knowing that even superheroes have their own problems, even if we regular folk can't get stabby with our demons when we want to.

The characters winning is *us* winning by association. We share solidarity with people we empathize with. That's why we watch and read. They are us and we are them.

It was only in my 40s that horror truly became an escape hatch as my life went completely south. *You're Next* (2011), *Midsommar* (2019), *28 Weeks Later* (2007), *Train to Busan* (2016), *Kingdom* (2019), and *The Walking Dead* (2010-2022) helped me see that there is great polarity in human nature. There will always be good and evil people, and the evil will never change. I have to learn how to see people for what they truly are. A new skill to acquire and hone at age 47. I am still learning.

I realize that to truly heal, I have to allow myself to feel those complicated and difficult emotions I'd blocked for decades: anger, rage, grief, sadness, disappointment, pride, joy.

After decades of not dreaming, dreams have slowly trickled back into my sleep. My brain is processing emotions again and this has lifted the incredible toll it had placed on my body.

I learned that if we don't process how we feel, our bodies will pay for it through chronic headaches, stomachaches, inflammation, tumors, and more. I don't like it, but it is what it is. My nightmares have transformed into a montage of chaotic dreamscapes and sometimes, they are even more horrific.

I have put them all down on paper.

Lately, I've been writing more about evil and the monsters in this world, reflecting what has afflicted all of us during this dark and dangerous season.

Will we survive this or is it the end of us? I don't know. There are too many iterations to calculate and far too many unknowns. Maybe we will get a Hail Mary in the end. Maybe we won't. But for certain, dark days are ahead of us.

And as they always have, writing and horror are slowly mending me, cushioning my falls, my pain seeping into the paper and screen, dissipating as they are transformed into fiction and poetry. They haven't completely healed me. I doubt they ever will.

But they have kept me from the edge, made me strong to be there for the people I love, helped me breathe and fight another day. Like the Final Girl drenched in blood, holding a well-used ax, I will endure long after the credits have rolled.

Women's Roles in Norse Stories: From the Edda to Tolkien to Marvel to Contemporary Fiction, Women Kick Ass in Norse Legends

BY JOHN TUTTLE

The ice moves majestically, irresistibly. Human effort is not futile, but man fights against the giant forces of Nature in a spirit of humility. One has a sense of dependence on the higher Power. — Sir Ernest Shackleton, polar explorer

When we ponder them, we think of their dragon-headed galleons striking fear into their opponents. We are quite familiar with their helmets sporting their distinct nose guards, and we admire the bravery of both male and female warriors among their communities.

They were some of the earliest of those travelers who ventured to the New World. They were seafarers. Their frigid, brutal homeland reared them up into fighters battered and shaped by the trials of survival. Their myths tell of Odin, Thor, and Loki. They are, of course, the Vikings—or, in a more broad sense—the Norse.

Their culture, their language, and their bold history have affected countless creatives. One of the places that Norse influence can be heavily detected is in the wide realm of literature. Nordic odors of symbolism and conceptualization can be found in everything from comic books to novels.

Classic Norse and Its Influence on Modern Storytelling

It is important to acknowledge first that the Norse wrote their own sagas. Many of their mythological musings were recounted in the Edda, a collection of Icelandic literature comprised of two sections: the *Younger Edda*, also known as the *Prose Edda* and the *Elder Edda*, also known as the *Poetic Edda*. Both segments, in written form, are dated approximately to the 13th century A.D.

We see plentiful ties in modern cultural works tracing back to various elements presented in the Edda. In a part of the Younger Edda, the *Gylfaginning*, the Norse gods inform King Gylfi of a number of things including Ragnarok, an event understood to be the doom of the gods.

Ragnarok and many other components of Norse mythology, as any geek knows, have trickled down into Marvel comics (Thor was introduced as a character there in the sixties) and into the MCU. The hysterically epic *Thor: Ragnarok* (2017) very much depicts what could be likened to a "doom of the gods" as the plot escalates toward Hela's devastation of Asgard.

Elements of the Edda have shaped other aspects of pop-cultural phenomena. Consider *The Lord of the Rings* (1954), an acclaimed body of literature as well as an astounding cinematic trilogy. Some of the common knowledge concerning Viking raiders and Norse myths makes it easier to notice a number of J.R.R. Tolkien's borrowed influences. A few generic examples would be the similarities between the Rohirrim's warfare and burial customs and the Vikings' and the similarities between character names such as Shadowfax and Goldfax, otherwise referred to as Gullfaxi.

On a worthwhile side note, Goldfax would also find modern rejuvenation in the Icelandic fairy tale "The Horse Gullfaxi and the Sword Gunnfoder" as included in *The Crimson Fairy Book* (1903) by Andrew Lang.

In 1969, a few years after Thor began showing up in Marvel comics, editor and author Lin Carter claimed to have discovered a slew of connections between Tolkien's Middle-earth saga and the Nordic Edda. Carter sees these connections as being far more obvious and direct than the correlations of Norse culture and Icelandic language perpetuated in Tolkien's epic. The critic's thesis may be summed up as follows:

"...elves, dragons, trolls, and dwarves—all of which are in Tolkien—can also be found in the tales of Grimm and Anderson: Tolkien did not invent them, he used them. But little else in the trilogy looks familiar at first glance. It is not until one takes a long, thoughtful, close look that one begins to see how Tolkien has drawn upon the old Norse and Germanic body of myths and tales and has reshaped their substance to his own purpose" (*Tolkien: A Look Behind "The Lord of the Rings"*, 157).

One of the most blatant comparisons Carter draws between the characters of Norse myth and those of Tolkien makes reference to *The Hobbit*, the children's book which served to set the stage for the later *Lord of the Rings* trilogy. He points out that Gandalf is far from an original name, that a figure known as King Gandalf of Vingulmark appears in the Icelandic Norse tale *Heimskringla*, which was written by Snorri Sturluson, the chieftain who authored the *Younger Edda*. The British author took a bunch of character names from the *Elder Edda* as well.

One of the highlights of Tolkien's epic is the role which Eowyn has to play in the grand scheme of things. In *The Lord of the Rings*, everyone has a function to fulfill—from Gollum on up to Aragorn. Eowyn is a chief example of one such character, specifically one without whom goodness could not have prevailed. It is at her hands in the midst of the battle that the Witch King of Angmar meets defeat—the terrible foe that *no man could kill*.

Tolkien weaves a depiction of a fair noblewoman who proves herself to be strong, bold, and heroic without ever diminishing her inherent beauty. This is the element you shall want to pay attention to: the role of women in a position of leadership and defense.

As we are going to see, it is a common theme spread throughout Norse-inspired fiction.

Women in Norse-Inspired Modern Literature

Tolkien was not the only writer of his day and age to be fascinated with Norse myths. Sigrid Undset, a writer from Norway, infused some of her work with Norse myths as well as Christian motifs. She specialized in historical fiction. Her acuity in expression through the written word led to Undset's winning of the Nobel Prize in Literature in 1928, making her the third woman to receive such an honor. Including Undset, only 15 women have received this award.

A slew of her works deal with Norwegian histories, and her novel *Gunnar's Daughter* (Penguin, 1909) is part of this tradition, with the plot taking place circa the tenth and eleventh centuries A.D. Undset's novel was published in 1909, a few years after Andrew Lang's *The Crimson Fairy Book*, and follows Vigdis Gunnarsdatter. The book weaves a drama with poignant elements of true love, courage, sexual assault, and comeback.

One appreciative reader of *Gunnar's Daughter* described the protagonist thus:

"I loved how strong a woman Vigdis was...but ultimately I was sad about how unforgiving and hard she remained over the course of her life and what this meant in terms of the people she loved."

It is this keen observation that brings us to a turning point in our examination of Nordic influence on modern literature: the role of women. In short, their role is significant. This fantastic literary notion is grounded in historical reality. While still members of a primarily male-dominated society, Norse women experienced a liberty and position which few women had seen since the ancient Egyptian culture. Abuse toward women came with a lawful penalty. Meanwhile, women would often handle familial finances and stand in charge of the homestead in the event of the husband's absence. Furthermore, there's evidence suggesting that there were female warrior Vikings in real life, though many scholars remain skeptical.

In the fashion of many a fantastical Norse-based adventure, women often represent game-changers, fighters, leaders. (Consider Odin's Valkeries in the old myths, for instance.) As we will see, many of the attributes Undset gave Vigdis are shared by other female characters in this tradition.

Aside from the Icelandic-influenced works of the early 20th century, there also exists a large amount of contemporary literature that focuses on Nordic characters and locales. Tolkien's Middle-earth saga and Marvel's comics dealing with "the gods" are a few examples. Yet, there are certainly more recent endeavors in this great literary tradition.

There is a host of 21st-century Sigrid Undsets as it were, women novelists who are striving toward presenting relatable revolutionaries through stories set in a past reminiscent of the Norse culture. One of these novelists is Cressida Cowell, author of the *How to Train Your Dragon* book series.

Like many exciting sagas, a loyal fandom has built itself around the books and the feature film adaptations. Since 2010, *How to Train Your Dragon* has been adapted into a number of films and series. In the 2014 film *How to Train Your Dragon 2*, movie audiences were introduced to Valka, the protagonist's mother who had been believed to be dead. (Coincidentally, Cate Blanchett—who played Hela in *Thor: Ragnarok* and Galadriel in *The Lord of the Rings* films—voices Valka.) However, Valka is not the same type of matriarchal figure we see in Vigdis or the other Norse matriarchs we'll be discussing.

Valka represents a virtuous, albeit troubled, woman seeking the greater good. In an attempt at achieving that collective good, she must make personal sacrifices. Specifically, she refrains from returning to her family in order to preserve an assumed peace between dragons and Vikings. It is years before she deems it appropriate to reconnect with her husband and her son.

This melodrama and conflict of calling is something that we do see in most of the Norse matriarchs of modern fantasy. However, Valka eventually comes to terms with her life choices. She is ever the warrior and defender, but once she finds Hiccup again, her role as a mother becomes the highlight of her existence. They wish to be a family reunited. Valka's personality is much more peace-loving and merciful than that of other matriarchs in her line of literary tradition.

Following after Cowell's success, Linnea Hartsuyker is another modern-day Sigrid Undset. Hartsuyker composed the *Golden Wolf* trilogy, beginning with the publication of *The Half-Drowned King* in 2017. Its sequel, *The Sea Queen*, appeared a year later, and the finalizing chapter of the saga was recounted in *The Golden Wolf* (2019). One of the primary themes this trilogy relates is the story of Svanhild Eysteinsson, a woman of honorable lineage, who takes on various roles of leadership such as commanding war vessels in *The Sea Queen*.

Once again, Svanhild's story is distraught with a hasty relationship which proves unhealthy, a passion for distant dreams, and an obligation to a heavy responsibility. Furthermore, Svanhild's natural agility and acuity as a seafarer must be duly noted. An avid traveler, a fighter, one who acts in authority and experience—Svanhild makes for a rather potent figure. Sister to King Harald of Norway, her title as "Sea Queen" is not merely honorary but is inseparably linked to a royal bloodline.

These same elements are found in the currently unfolding *Book of Bera* trilogy (2017-2019) by Suzie Wilde. Wilde's protagonist is, not too surprisingly, a courageous Viking woman. She is named Bera—a pioneer, a mother, a protector, a mystic, and a leader. She has obviously got a lot of stuff she's trying to balance simultaneously. Things only become more clouded and complex when the fate of her people's future rests on her shoulders. This responsibility beckons of a vocation perceived toward leadership, specifically to providing and caring for her people. Ottar, Bera's father, inspired this inclination within her through his offering of time and talents to those whom he cared for.

The *Book of Bera* saga has thus far been set down in the first two volumes: *Sea Paths* (2017) and *Obsidian* (2019), not to mention the climactic close to the saga in store for the future. Bera's story becomes doubly intriguing as she is often involved with sensing danger on a more spiritual plane of existence. In *Obsidian*, one of the underlying emotions with which Bera is flooded at various intervals is the keen attraction to returning to the lifestyle of a sea-rider. She is being drawn to the ocean, much like Legolas sings of a longing for the sea in *The Return of the King*. Bera wants to go back to a seafaring of the magnitude and essence of Svanhild's.

As with Tolkien, many of these leading female roles are derived from Norse mythological characters. For instance, Bera's father may have been influenced by the Norse mythological character Óttar, who was associated with the goddess Freya. For our purposes, Freya shall be the mythological figure who, more than any other, serves as the principal prototype for the matriarchs depicted in so many of the works mentioned above.

Freya was the most iconic, most lauded goddess of the Norse tales. In examining her genealogy and various functions as portrayed in mythology, we can easily see how the aura of Freya's personality rubs off on many of the female protagonists in the modern Norse-esque epics.

Freya is a goddess of love, fertility, battle, and death. Already this sums up much of what we have analyzed in the Norse-inspired literary protagonists of the past century or more. The protagonists are frequently love-stricken as in the case of Bera and Vigdis. We look at Bera and Valka and see how their maternal instincts stretch far and wide—from bringing new life into the world and caring for children to watching out for the community as a whole. We look to Eowyn and Svanhild, and we see their manifestation as warriors, cheerers, and defenders. Furthermore, the mythological father of Freya was Njörd, god of the sea. This may explain the keen fascination and longing which so many of the matriarchs have for the sea. Being out on the tumultuous, fickle waves makes them feel at home.

In regards to creative approach, one should notice that these female-led novels are nearly all authored by women. This only seems natural as writers primarily craft their protagonists after themselves. These authors are projecting their own aspirations, potential, and concerns into the characters and the stories which they create.

A theme that comes up more than once is that of sexual harassment and abuse with women fighting against victimization. Certainly, some of this is serving to offer a social commentary of our own times. Ours is a world that continues to be ravaged by a culture of objectification prone to abuse, and we hear about instances of such abuse frequently. This is an element deeply rooted in Sigrid Undset's *Gunnar's Daughter* and can also be glimpsed briefly in the *Book of Bera* saga. In *Obsidian*, as Bera is making her way through the congested throngs of people, she is harassed by a mini mob.

Moreover, the overarching theme of all these stories is to prove to the reader the merit and potential of women as being equal to those of men. In looking at many of these stories, such as *How to Train Your Dragon* or the *Book of Bera*, it is through the welcomed cooperation between men and women, requiring humility and strength from both, that great deeds are accomplished. The final takeaway is that women deserve a share in authoritative roles. These stories strive to show that women are perfectly capable of tackling larger-than-life troubles, approaching them from a unique perspective, and overcoming them.

The historical Nordic people explored new lands as we now explore new literature, sailing ever onward headed for a brighter tomorrow. We have seen the significant Norse influences which linger into some of the most recent works of contemporary fiction. From their legacy has sprung forth works of juvenile fiction which resonate with the child in all of us as well as works which endeavor to draw attention to stark societal dilemmas such as the handling of abuse and equality pertaining to roles of responsibility.

In conclusion, the Norse lifestyle and their mythological records have served as a foundation for some of the most inspirational literature of the 20th and 21st centuries.

Women of Science Fiction and Fantasy Television: 70 Years of Reaching for the Stars

BY KAREN A. ROMANKO

"Throughout the history of television, women have played changing roles in science fiction and fantasy, from Xena to Buffy to Star Trek and beyond."

When television first went to the stars in series such as *Space Patrol* (1950–1955) and *Tom Corbett, Space Cadet* (1950–1955), women joined the action, piloting rocketships, contributing scientific innovations, and moving tentatively beyond the role of damsel in distress. When Vena Ray (Sally Mansfield) crashes the gate at the Office of Space Affairs in "Beyond the Curtain of Space," a 1954 episode of *Rocky Jones, Space Ranger*, she pushes her way onto an important mission, whether Rocky Jones (Richard Crane) wants her there or not. While Vena's fictional action was an auspicious start for women on SFF TV, later progress occurred in fits and starts, as networks and creators became more conservative once big bucks could be made (and lost) on the burgeoning medium.

In my book *Women of Science Fiction and Fantasy Television: An Encyclopedia of 400 Characters and 200 Shows, 1950–2016* (McFarland, 2019), I chart the changing depictions of female characters throughout seven decades of SFF television, focusing especially on their jobs, costumes, racial and ethnic diversity, sexual orientation, and age. I found that the march toward modern viewpoints was sometimes hampered by the prejudices of the creators themselves, but also by TV networks and series sponsors, who often tapped the brakes on enlightened presentations due to concern about offending audiences.

A decade after *Rocky Jones, Space Ranger* premiered, women were still traveling to the stars in shows such as *Lost in Space* (1965–1968) and *Star Trek* (1966–1969). While we might have expected female characters to continue the tradition of working as pilots and scientists, the two most prominent women in *Star Trek*, Lieutenant Uhura (Nichelle Nichols) and Nurse Chapel (Majel Barrett) worked in traditionally "female" occupations, a "glorified telephone operator" to use Nichelle Nichols's own words, and a nurse. Barrett, in fact, had earlier been cast as the second in command of the USS Enterprise in the 1964 pilot for the series, "The Cage." Her character, known simply as Number One, had been a pants-wearing, logical command officer, who was one step away from the captain's chair. NBC rejected this pilot, and when the *Star Trek* we know whooshed across our TV screens in 1966, the featured women were further down the chain of command, and wore micro-miniskirts with matching panties as their uniforms. It would take 30 years for Star Trek's TV franchise to produce a female starship captain via Voyager's Kathryn Janeway (Kate Mulgrew), and, yes, she wore pants.

The original *Star Trek* had taken a true step forward, however, by including an African-American woman, Uhura, as part of the Enterprise's bridge crew. Lieutenant Uhura was one of the first African-American characters to be featured in a non-stereotypical role on US television, moving beyond the traditional role of domestic servant. Although her character was groundbreaking, Uhura herself often didn't have much to do in each episode beyond reciting the now iconic phrase "hailing frequencies open." As a result, Nichols had planned to leave the series for a Broadway career after the first season, but an unlikely source, none other than Dr. Martin Luther King, Jr., convinced Nichols to stay, emphasizing that her character sent a positive message of racial equality in the future.

While women in 60s space operas were not at the top of cast rosters, their sisters in fantasy sitcoms found lead roles in shows set in the domestic sphere, far away from the "manly" realms of outer space. Among others, Elizabeth Montgomery starred as a witch who tried to adapt to a suburban life with a mortal husband in *Bewitched* (1964–1972), while Barbara Eden portrayed a genie who fell in love with her astronaut "master" in *I Dream of Jeannie* (1965- 1970).

It would be another decade before women emerged as leads in SFF action series, coinciding with the arrival of the second wave of feminism, a.k.a. the Women's Liberation Movement. Shows such as *Wonder Woman* (1975–1979), starring Lynda Carter, and *The Bionic Woman* (1976- 1978), with Lindsay Wagner, featured gorgeous women, who were sweet as apple pie and slender (never brawny), but they got to engage in modest action, which was something new, especially on American television.

Women of color would not become series leads until the 90s, a watershed period for women on SFF television. Early progress occurred on cable and syndicated series, such as *Beyond Reality* (1991–1993), with African-American actress Shari Belafonte as a ghostbusting professor, while Tia Carrere starred in *Relic Hunter* (1999–2002) as an archaeologist and adventurer a la Indiana Jones.

In the new millennium, actresses of color emerged as lead characters on the major networks, albeit sporadically. Jessica Alba, an actress of Mexican-American descent, starred in the Fox network series *Dark Angel* (2000–2002) as a genetically enhanced supersoldier, while Oscar-winner Halle Berry brought her movie-star wattage to the small screen in the CBS series *Extant* (2014–2015). Nicole Beharie portrayed Abbie Mills, a police lieutenant called upon to fight the coming apocalypse in Fox's *Sleepy Hollow* (2013- 2017). Although a popular and iconic character, Beharie's Mills was written out of the series after the third season, shocking and disappointing fans, who noticed that *Sleepy Hollow* had diminished its roles for actors of color since the first season.

Lesbian and bisexual characters gained prominence at the turn of the 21st Century after some implied appearances during the 1990s. Xena (Lucy Lawless) and Gabrielle (Renee O'Connor) had been constant companions in *Xena: Warrior Princess,* (1995- 2001), but a sexual relationship was never depicted on screen, although many fans had assumed (and even insisted) it was there. Similar assumptions were made about Susan Ivanova (Claudia Christian) of *Babylon 5* (1994–1998), who hosted a sleepover for Talia Winters (Andrea Thompson), but had disappeared during the night, leaving matters to viewers' imaginations.

In the next decade, lesbian and bisexual relationships weren't just implied—they were clearly depicted. *Buffy the Vampire Slayer* (1997–2003) had introduced the apparently straight character of Willow Rosenberg (Alyson Hannigan) in 1997, but starting in 2000, Willow had embarked upon a love affair with fellow witch Tara Maclay (Amber Benson), culminating in a watershed on-screen kiss in "The Body" (2001). *Lost Girl* (2010–2016) chronicled the adventures of pansexual succubus Bo Dennis (Anna Silk), who learned self-control from her lover Lauren Lewis (Zoie Palmer), so she wouldn't accidentally kill her partners during sexual encounters. *The 100* (2014-) featured the first bisexual lead on network TV in Clarke Griffin (Eliza Taylor), but created controversy when Griffin's female lover was killed, a victim of "dead lesbian syndrome," many thought, a TV affliction wherein lesbian characters meet too frequent demises (as had Buffy's Tara).

In 2015, ABC brought *Agent Carter*, a spin-off from the film *Captain America: The First Avenger*, to the small screen. Peggy Carter (Hayley Atwell), a character set in the 40s, but depicted in the new millennium, was perfectly placed to comment on the history of women on and off television in the postwar years. She often highlighted the sexism of her colleagues, even if the word "sexism" wasn't used in that era, but one speech, in particular, transcended the rest. "You think you know me, but I've never been more than what each of you has created. To you, I'm the stray kitten, left on your doorstep to be protected. The secretary turned damsel in distress. The girl on the pedestal, transformed into some daft whore."

Peggy Carter reminds us of where we've been. While we note the undeniable progress women have made over the last 70 years in portraying characters ever more substantive and diverse, we can't ignore the subtle steps backward that often accompany their progress. As women continue to reach for the stars on SFF television, let's not forget the women and the lessons of the past.

The Spectre of Trauma: How Ghost Stories Reflect Humanity's Struggle with Mental Health

BY LAURA DÍAZ DE ARCE

Part 1: Dead Men DO Tell Tales

Crimson Peak (2015) ends in a bittersweet goodbye between Thomas (Tom Hiddleston) and Edith (Mia Wasikowska). Thomas, already dead and a ghost, seems to acquiesce to Edith's plea and distracts his sister Lucille (Jessica Chastain) long enough for Edith to kill her. It's interesting that the film portrays Thomas as someone sympathetic to the audience, considering he aided and acted in all of Lucille's crimes. Lucille then becomes a ghost to haunt Crimson Peak as well. All of those who passed away in Crimson Peak become ghosts—because pain can easily mark a landscape.

As a child, I loved ghost stories. The ones I found the most frustrating were those that removed ghosts from whatever history they had. Stories that gave no reason for why the ghost was the way they were. Rather, these stories, or books, or movies, focused on the living protagonists dealing with identity-less spirits. This always struck me as shallow. I wanted reason—perhaps I knew even then that people, dead or alive, rarely acted without some sort of prompting. What drove them to haunt? Who were these ghosts as people? In many ways, I wanted to know what hurt them, and what caused them to hurt in return.

That may have been why *Crimson Peak* was as satisfying a film as it was to me. Each ghost has a reason for being, each a reason for their continued pain. Even the villains get some background as to why they act as they do. Lucille and Thomas raised in isolation by a neglectful and abusive mother gives their pain some context, even if it doesn't excuse their behavior.

Before we continue in this discussion, I'm going to ask for a few favors. First, I'm going to ask that you have a little sympathy for the devil, and that you reserve forming strict good/bad dualities on some characters that will be discussed, as the nature of these stories naturally involve some type of violence. Secondly, I'm going to ask that you think about pain, about the nature of pain and how it manifests, it festers, and is transferred.

Ghosts, whether fictional or folkloric, are trauma expressed in physical or metaphysical form. We can use ghosts as a way to discuss, explore, and confront different types of trauma. For this piece, we'll mostly focus on films and tv, but this can be appropriated to any ghost media and representation.

Haunted houses are particularly popular displays in how trauma can root people into place. *Crimson Peak* has Edith experiencing the trauma of resident ghosts (Thomas' murdered wives). There have also been a number of analysis written on trauma in Netflix's *The Haunting of Hill House*, including *Jade Eby's "Unpacking the Trauma in 'The Haunting of Hill House'" on Medium*. These discussions often focus on the living protagonists confronting either their own trauma or transcending the resident ghosts trauma. I'm less concerned with the living, in this case, than with the dead.

Trauma and Mental Health

When you work in mental health or are involved with the mental health community, trauma becomes secondhand conversation. In Peer Work[1] we often try to adhere to trauma-informed care—in other words, we try to work from the assumption that whoever we are working with has experienced some sort of trauma. This assumption turns out to be largely correct the majority of the time, as the more we study about trauma, the more we discover that it is *a large cause of mental health issues.*

For those that have experienced trauma, it is a living thing. It can evolve, and change and comes in many different shades. In mental health, for instance, we may talk about ACEs (*Adverse Childhood Experiences*) that range from physical abuse to living in poverty, neglect, etc. Having one or more ACE can create poor outcomes for the person who experienced them, leading to things like mental illness, substance misuse, chronic disease, and early death. That is not to say that everyone with a high amount of ACEs will have poor outcomes, or will be unable to work through those outcomes. But we know that trauma is hard on the body. People with an ACEs score of six or more, even when adjusted for health and socio-economic factors, can have a mortality rate *reduced by up to twenty years.*

Bringing this back to ghosts, it becomes obvious how ghosts are representative of trauma. They are often made by traumatic events (murders, death by exposure, etc). There's also the ironic deniability of trauma. We can't always see the effects of trauma in things outside of physical scars, we can't always read it on an EKG or an MRI, but it most certainly has a physical presence for the person with it.

Ghosts aren't only trauma, they are also representative of the ways that trauma is self-replicating.

In the 2007 film *El Orfanato*, both Laura (Belén Rueda) and son Simon (Roger Príncep) end up dying to make up for the sins of the past, a sin that Laura is only tangentially related to, having resided in the same orphanage where all the children were murdered. First, the ghosts lure Simon to cause his death, which leads to Laura's suicide. *El Orfanato* is a film with a happy ending. Laura ends up running an orphanage for dead children, and these ghosts now have someone to take care of them. This does not negate the very real violence inherent in those acts to begin with. But what is unique about this ghost movie is how it frames this violence, as done by child ghosts desperate for affection.

Rather than simply condemn the act of luring a child to his death and haunting a woman to suicide, it also understands that these acts were made in a history of cruelty. That those children were reenacting their own histories, in an effort to find safety and security.

In mental health, we often work with people who are largely abuse and trauma victims; those who have complex adverse experiences. Though it bears repeating that people with mental illness are no more violent than the general population, they are *more likely to experience violence,* and the "victim-to-victimizer" cycle is largely overblown[2]. Every once in a while, you may work with someone who has perpetrated violence. They may have assaulted and abused someone. When you look into their past, often you will find some set of trauma.

It strikes me as cruel to expect people raised in violence to be totally devoid of that violence. In that same vein, it is cruel to be upset at "ghosts" when they haunt, when they enact such violence. Like those ghostly orphans, we sometimes re-enact our traumas because it can become our best language. Sometimes we don't realize that we cannot get rid of our pain by giving pain to someone else.

Part 2: Our Unfinished Business

While I loved ghost stories, I was never much for scary movies. Things got especially more difficult after I left a two-year abusive relationship. Every time I watched a film where someone was trapped or being followed, it took me back to that time. I would feel pulled under, back to when a life where I felt like I had to watch everything I said or did to avoid a blowup. It was a time when I felt as helpless as a victim in a ghost story, waiting for something to pop out and drag me down.

The fact that ghosts often have haunts—either an object, place, or a person—is fitting in discussions of trauma. Traumatic events and experiences can root someone in time, or have them repeating it over and over again.

Returning to *The Haunting of Hill House*, we can see Nell's (Victoria Pedretti) trauma is one that time travels. She is haunted by the "Bent-Neck Lady" as a child which turns out to be her future after she completes suicide. For people who suffer from Post-Traumatic Stress Disorder (*1*), certain triggers can cause the past to become present, forcing us to relive our traumas in vivid detail. It is only when we confront these ghosts or excise them, that we remove this repetitive pain.

The premise in many ghost stories is that ghosts are here due to unfinished business. Ghosts can therefore be excised when this business is completed. This commonly necessitates three steps:

1. The ghost or haunting is acknowledged
2. The ghost's history is uncovered as well as whatever tasks need completion
3. The task is completed, and the ghost(s) move on

One of the most popular movies that really displayed this to any effect was M. Night Shyamalan's *The Sixth Sense* (1999). Despite the fact that Shyamalan's portrayal of disabled people is often extremely stigmatizing, here we have an example where ghosts are given back their humanity. Cole's (Haley Joel Osment) gift of seeing the dead is at first dismissed, but when he and Malcolm (Bruce Willis) acknowledge it's a possibility, that opens the door for Cole to confront the issue. This allows him to respond to the ghost Kyra (Mischa Barton) without fear, and investigate her death. They reveal how her mother poisoned her and create the possibility of justice. Kyra can move on, and eventually, so can Malcolm.

This same set of steps can also be used in dealing with trauma:

1. We have to acknowledge that the trauma took place and that it has resonance.
2. Next, we may want to trace the effects of that trauma, and what may be needed to cope.
3. Finally, we have to accept that trauma is a part of our lives, but it does not have to rule it.

All of this is largely more difficult that excising a poltergeist or a spirit, but at least, it lets us understand the ways in which we might be able to confront our own hauntings.

The 2001 horror film *The Others* is unique in that it is from the point of view of ghosts, haunted not just by the living intruders, but by other spirits and their past. Grace (Nicole Kidman) spends the majority of the film in denial of what she sees and observes as well as the truth of what she has to confront. She does not want to admit to killing her children in panic, nor her suicide. The residual peace comes from the acknowledgment that the violence took place, and the acceptance of her new (after) living situation. She must accept the violence that happened, what it has done to her and her children, but at the same time, it is foreshadowed she can now carve out an existence with the children she wronged.

There is no real, "moving on" in *The Others*, only the moving forward. The same can be said for trauma. Grace becomes a fascinating study, in that she is a combination of a perpetrator of such violence, a victim of it, and one that transcends the torture of both. She may have made these ghosts, but that does not end her agency.

When I am not well, I am reminded about how I was before I got treatment for my mental illness. There were times when I experienced a mixed episode or came down from mania, where I sometimes said hurtful things to people I cared about. I think about the pain I caused when I was in pain. These memories are the ghosts that haunt me, joined by other traumas, but I worry about the ghosts I have given others in my own anger. I used to obsess about the ghosts I gave others with flippant carelessness. Accepting these ghosts has been part of my recovery process—I cannot banish them to the ether no more than I could seance a spirit. At least, to paraphrase *The Others*, "The living and the dead can learn to live together."

As for the haunted presence of my ex? It's still there, and the panic still comes and goes when I've run into someone that looks like him or when I watch someone stroll through a haunted house. I don't forgive him, but I hope that he's learned not to leave a poltergeist behind. No one is immune to causing pain, but maybe, maybe with a little less skepticism, we can begin to heal and let something else grow out of our pain, like flowers at a gravestone.

This article originally appeared in the *Bronzeville Bee*.

---

1. *A Peer Specialist is a certifiable position in a number of states, the purpose of which is to increase empowerment, advocacy, and education. In Florida, Peer Specialists have to have lived experience with mental illness and/or substance misuse disorder. There are additional peers certifications such as those for Military Veterans, Parents and relatives of those with mental health issues and/or substance misuse, and childhood experience. Peers can serve a number of functions in systems of care such as "coaches" to individuals, lead groups, run respite houses, or perform in-hospital advocacy guidance.*
2. *Glasser, M. & Kolvin, I & Campbell, D & Glasser, A & Leitch, I & Farrelly, S. (2002) Cycle of Child Sexual Abuse: Links Between Being a Victim and Becoming a Perpetrator. The British Journal of Psychiatry: The Journal of Mental Science. 179. 482–94; Discussion 495. 10.1192/BJP.179.6.482.*

Oppression and Slavery in Speculative Short Fiction: Contemporary Black Writers Dive into History

BY NATHAN ELIAS

"We must utilize the art and ideas created by these writers as tools for enlightenment and lenses through which we can identify, and with which we can contribute to, much needed social change."

In the Foreword to *New Suns: Original Speculative Fiction by People of Color* (*Rebellion*, 2019), LeVar Burton says, "[W]e continually create the world we occupy—in our imaginations first, and only afterwards do we make those visions manifest in this world...[O]ur exploration into the unknown should cause us to examine who we are as sentient beings, and science fiction as a tool for social change makes for a most welcome companion on our journey."

This point in time is one ripe for examination. With the resurgence of the public's awareness of systemic racism and Black oppression in the United States, and because atrocities are still being committed against Black Americans, it is imperative to read speculative fiction by Black writers. These works help us empathize with and imagine the effects of systemic racism and oppression.

Highlighted in this article are two contemporary short works of speculative fiction by Black writers: Rivers Solomon's story, "Blood is Another Word for Hunger" (a 2020 Hugo Award Finalist) and Phenderson Djèlí Clark's "The

Secret Lives of the Nine Negro Teeth of George Washington" (winner of the 2018 Nebula Award). By taking a closer look at these stories, the roots of Black oppression in the United States—namely slavery—can be viewed through a speculative lens.

In "Blood is Another Word for Hunger", an enslaved girl named Sully is pushed to the brink of madness after her master is killed in battle. Sully is so devastated by his death that she murders her master's family—"the family who'd raised her"—in their sleep. While it might be easy to question why a slave would be so negatively impacted by the death of her master, speculative fiction writer Tananarive Due notes in her essay in *Octavia's Brood: Science Fiction Stories from Social Justice Movements (AK Press, 2015)*:

> *"The intricate social webs between the racial groups during the practice of slavery have never been purely black and white. For example, ...most slaves did not run away...[Sometimes], no matter how uncomfortable the notion, there was...genuine affection for slave masters, a kind of systemic Stockholm Syndrome that those of us who haven't experienced slavery will never understand."*

Due notes that Stockholm Syndrome is one of several reasons slaves may have chosen to not escape; she offers a strong motive for the character of Sully. However, Sully's choice to murder her master's family out of the pain she feels from losing her master is far from the story's primary speculative concern; Solomon's speculative elements pertain to what the story's narrator refers to as "the etherworld", from which Sully births a ghost-like revenant for every life she takes.

The first and most important revenant birthed by Sully is a young woman named Ziza; Ziza serves as a friend, lover, and sister-figure to Sully. Ziza convinces Sully that they can live in her old master's home: "Did you not kill the folks who had the papers [to the home]? Therefore could you not change the papers? Is an owner anything but he who kills for the papers?"

Sully soon births more revenants for each of the members of her master's family she killed, but she soon realizes their small brood isn't enough; Sully decides to kill more people in order to birth more revenants and strengthen their growing clan. The killing escalates into a battle with the townspeople, but in the end, even after victory, Sully learns that her thirst can never be quenched. She is taught how to be happy—only after having taken her own life and being born again through her own womb—from Ziza through the sweetness of song.

Solomon's choice of content revolving around slavery and their speculative conceit about birthing revenants per persons killed begs the question: Where does the trauma of slavery end? As Due notes in her *Octavia's Brood* essay, "the moral dilemma all blacks face in their examination of [their] past in slavery [is that]...after generations of heartache and discrimination, Black Americans...were ultimately the beneficiaries of slavery." Solomon's story looks back to the birth of this inheritance and, metaphorically, examines how its psychological effects inescapably manifest.

Phenderson Djèlí Clark's story, unlike Rivers Solomon's, is deliberately concerned with slavery's historical narrative in the United States, making characters of the first U.S. President and nine slaves from whom he acquired teeth.

The structure of "The Secret Lives of the Nine Negro Teeth of George Washington" is straightforward: the narrative begins with the "first Negro tooth purchased for George Washington," or the first Black person Washington ever took a tooth from, and ends with the ninth person and final tooth. Clark riffs on the popular lore of Washington paying slaves for teeth that were likely used in his dentures, and in doing so he renders an alternate history filled with magic, conjurers, sorcerers, lycanthropes, necromancers, and innocent dreamers. He briefly recounts the life of each person, how they came to be in a position of having a tooth sold to Washington, and how Washington regarded the tooth.

Not all of the slaves in Clark's story are of Earthly origins: "The sixth Negro tooth of George Washington belonged to a slave who had tumbled here from another world." This "conjured Negro" is "bundled up and shipped from London to a slave market" at Mount Vernon, Virginia. The slave is given the name Esther and later has premonitions about agriculture and the weather that always come true, which impresses her plantation manager. Later, the narrator explains that, when wearing Esther's tooth, Washington would dream of "golden spires and colorful glass domes, where Negroes flew through the sky on metal wings like birds and sprawling cities that glowed bright at night and were run by machines who thought faster than men."

The story of the ninth tooth follows a girl named Emma who, unlike the other eight, has no supernatural traits. What makes her special is that she dreams to live in a place "where she might draw a free breath and taste its sweetness." These dreams work their own magic and are transmitted to Washington when he wears Emma's tooth; according to the narrator, Emma's dreams of freedom are the reason he frees 123 of his slaves in Djèlí Clark's story.

The central theme of "The Nine Negro Teeth of George Washington" can be found in its first paragraph: "[W]hen you make a man or woman a slave you enslave yourself in turn. And the souls of those who made thralls of others would never know rest—in this life, or the next."

Djèlí Clark's theme of the negative karmic values bestowed upon slavers and Solomon's theme of the seemingly bottomless trauma of slavery illuminate heightened origins of Black oppression in the United States, which are still being felt hundreds of years later. On one hand, Djèlí Clark's story shows us how the mystification of the United States' history of slavery allows for easily blurred facts (such as how it is often left out that George Washington acquired and wore teeth from Black slaves) and downright lies. Similarly, today we see some people aiming to mystify systemic racism as if it is not an ongoing byproduct of slavery.

Just as Djèlí Clark's themes imply, the price of this suffering must be paid by someone; the question is: why must Black Americans continue to pay for crimes committed against them? On the other hand, Solomon's story shows us that the intrinsic damage—oppression—done to Black Americans as a result of slavery cannot be undone without drastic measures; in fact, even after drastic measures are taken, the cyclical effects continue to exist.

Just as LeVar Burton suggests, it is our job, through reading speculative writing by Black writers such as Djèlí Clark and Solomon, to examine who we are as sentient beings in relation to slavery in the United States. We must utilize the art and ideas created by these writers as tools for enlightenment and lenses through which we can identify, and with which we can contribute to, much needed social change.

In Defense of Bad Horror Movies: Lesbian Vampire Films & Re-Examining the Problematic

BY HOLLY LYN WALRATH

May 27, 1968 Paris, France.

For the month of May in 1968, Paris was barricaded by a slew of student protests. The protests began when a newly-constructed school reopened, crowding over 12,000 students into a hastily-constructed college. Student protests spiraled into labor strikes as more people took up the call of inequality. Businesses shut down and the city went quiet until May 27, when the Grenelle Agreements concluded, guaranteeing a rise in the minimum wage.

On that same date, audiences crowded into theatres to see the only film released during the chaos — *Le Viol du Vampire* (The Rape of the Vampire). The titillating name of the film, which was marketed as erotic horror, promised fans of the popular fantastique genre a thrilling romp.

These were audiences accustomed to the famed films by Hammer Film Productions—commercial renditions of classic books featuring Frankenstein and Dracula. Campy, often exploitative, and uncomplicated in plot. What French audiences got instead in the work of director Jean Rollin was a poetic exploration into the surreal, where women vampires controlled men and haunted girls went wandering through lonesome beaches. In response, some audiences rioted, uprooting seats and damaging theaters so badly that in one city the police had to be called.

It wasn't that audiences weren't prepared for lesbian vampires. They weren't prepared for a b-movie to be art.

A few years ago I discovered the work of Jean Rollin. I'm convinced I single-handedly made his movies only available for purchase on Amazon (they used to be free on Prime) because I watched them so much. My spouse and I call them "lesbian vampire movies" in jest.

Rollin's films were deemed b-movies (low-budget films that ran counterpart to "a-movies") at the time of their release. They had little to no budget, sometimes no script, and virtually no sets other than natural landscapes and strange villas. Because of this, they are in some ways clever and downright fascinating from a cinematography standpoint. They're obscure, little-known, sometimes strangely pornographic movies that explore common horror tropes like vampires and the undead. Rollin's films often featured porn stars. Despite all their bad movie aspects, I love them.

The Rape of the Vampire was Rollin's first feature film. He claims he didn't go into cinema to make erotica/horror. He was a lover of art and literature, and particularly a fan of American serials and comic books. Serving in the French military, he made army commercials before moving to low-budget films.

On the surface, the films of Jean Rollin look like shoddy, made for mock-a-thon, less-than-bad films. And some of them *are* bad. But their badness is what makes them compelling.

What I love about Rollin's horror films is their reversal of expectations. The female leads are leads (not sidekicks) and they are complicated villains. Male characters are often demoralized or terrorized by these seductress demon women. Rollin pokes fun at men who are tempted by the women's seduction, only to be killed at the hands of their temptation. The femme fatales of Rollin's fantastique world are folkloric, powerful, and immortal. They may be standing on a coffin nude, but you can bet they won't be leaving this world that way.

Growing up, I was a fan of *Scream* and the classic horror films of my generation that featured The Final Girl. My friends *were* the guys from *Scream*, sitting around discussing the genre and its tropes (and which leading ladies were naked in which film), oblivious to the sexism going on around them.

Rollin's films make the final girls the villains. Their motivations are murky; it is often unclear why they are hunting down men with a scythe (other than, hey, that's just damn cool.) For the final girl as villain, the horror lies not in how they got there or how they will escape, but what they are going to do to get revenge.

I can also acknowledge their sexploitation aspects. Rollin is the king of putting a beautiful naked woman in a fascinating setting. The male gaze is in full display mode. Rollin admitted that much of the erotic side of his films was encouraged by producers who thought sex sold. But the nudity in Rollin's films becomes akin to say, the surrealist visions of Goya, Paul Delvaux, or Leonor Fini. It is used to effect, often one that leans toward art, not porn.

Later in life, Rollin was hired to direct hardcore porn films under pseudonyms. They were tame for today's standards but at the time a part of a larger and thriving industry in France that was often censored. Featuring lesbian lovers, sex cults, captured virgins, and intense orgies, Rollin would have had very little control over these films despite being Director. In his early days, he was rumored to leave the set during the sex scenes because they made him uncomfortable (1).

It was these films that would gain him negative connotations in the industry, effectively wiping out much of the impact of his "personal" films (Most of his surrealist films were self-financed.) This misconception persisted throughout Rollin's life, and there was even a rumor that he sold women to sex rings (as far as I can learn, it was just a salacious rumor as most of the actresses in Rollin's films seem to have enjoyed working with him.)[1]

His most hated film is perhaps *Zombie Lake* (1981), in which a troop of Nazi soldiers are murdered by local villagers and later re-animated to terrorize the village. The movie opens with a skinny dipping scene and features some truly terrible makeup work for the zombies. While many have reviled the film, I actually found it weirdly touching as one of the soldiers reunites with his child in a complex story, if you think about the politics at hand.

Rollin and many horror filmmakers thought of women as objects. "For me, a naked girl is more interesting, for sensuality and for poetry (a naked girl is *always* poetry), to put her in a clock or in a chimney, or anywhere except a bed. Using things for unexpected uses is the base of all surrealist painting" (Jean Rollin, Interview in Kinoeye). I'm not sure I disagree with Rollin here, while I can still acknowledge that to compare a woman to a "thing" is eye-rollingly weak. Despite the cringe factor, it's true that to put women in danger gives the audience a kind of thrill. To see them escape that danger makes us emotionally tied to their existence. To see them survive gives us hope.

Like Rollin, my own writing is much heavier on the image than the story. Perhaps that's why I love so-called bad horror movies. They rely on instinct, on humor, and evocative, often bizarre imagery. They defy genre, doing things no right-minded director would dare. They often have to use emotion to greater effect than say, a mainstream film. As Rollin puts it, "For me, it's impossible to make "gore" without emotion. If there is no love, passion, there is no film" (Jean Rollin, Interview with Mondo Digital).

These days our culture spends a lot of time "canceling" bad media. And while I think there's a need for this sometimes, particularly when a film causes harm, I also often feel like shitty movies are a guilty pleasure. By the time a film has been made, it's our role as consumers and critics to comment on it. We're afraid to admit that we went to see a movie everyone hated just to see what all the hubbub is about.

And I think that it's okay to want to read, watch, or consume a media so that you have the knowledge to criticize it. When I was watching bad movies as a teen, I was learning what I loved, and that what I loved didn't have to be perfect.

In fact, the less perfect, the better.

---

1. *Fascination: The Celluloid Dreams of Jean Rollin*, by David Hinds, World Head Press, 2016.

Reviews

Netflix's Dark and the Art of Letting Go: Untangling the Labyrinth

BY ARCHITA MITTRA

The circularity of time travel becomes the perfect metaphor to depict the cycles of toxic relationships and familial abuse and show how the participants, no matter how unwilling, are often too helpless and afraid to break the cycle.

Dark (2020) is a trippy science fiction series currently streaming on Netflix that uses time travel to explore and unspool the entangled knot of human relationships.

It also draws inspiration from the tragic tale of the princess Ariadne. In one version of the Greek myth, Ariadne guides Theseus, the king of Athens, to the heart of a labyrinth and gives him a bronze sword to slay the Minotaur, trailing a spool of dark-red thread so that he isn't lost. Like most heroes, Theseus succeeds with a woman's help and promises to love her, only to later betray and abandon her in an island far away from home.

In the wake of the pandemic in 2020 the story of Ariadne and *Dark* suddenly felt *personal*. I was in my last semester at college, on the way to complete my master's degree in English Literature, with a fairly active social life and dreams of a successful career. Suddenly, I was plunged into isolation for months on end. I lost my job, fell out with a couple of friends I cared about deeply, had my heart broken and realized my writing career was going nowhere. Like the Cretan princess who fell in love with Theseus at first sight and betrayed her father and country to elope with him, only to be rejected and discarded like a worn-out tool, I too felt like I'd staked everything for a future that was never to be, with nothing to fall back on.

My mental health plummeted and I wandered through the labyrinth of my own past, contemplating my choices and mistakes, over and over, unable to find a way out. I felt hopeless and powerless. At this point, watching the German tv show *Dark*, that invoked Ariadne's tale like a leitmotif, felt like a harsh lesson in knowing when to give up everything for something that you believe in and when to let go forever.

The series is set in the fictional German town of Winden, where a man commits suicide on the same day a young child disappears near the town's mysterious caves. Soon dead bodies show up, more people disappear, and as the police struggle to solve the mystery, the show starts to switch back and forth in time. Different characters soon begin to time-travel either with a device or using the hidden passageways within the caves, with the hope of restoring things to normalcy, only to get entangled in deeper mysteries and time-paradoxes.

Much of the series follows Jonas Kahnwald, a teenager who grapples with the truth of his father's suicide, his crush on fellow classmate Martha, and his involvement in the mystery of the missing kids. It leads him down an unending rabbit hole of secrets, slowly stripping him of all agency, where he realizes that much of his future is already pre-determined. In his desperation to break the cycle of time travel, he becomes the very thing he hates, a murderer and manipulator. Although a *timey wimey* love story at its heart, *Dark* is more concerned with parental abuse, cheating spouses and children turning on their parents, in an unending cycle of betrayal and toxic love.

Presenting itself as a puzzle to be solved, the show befuddles viewers with its intertwined family tree and time loops, luring us deeper into the fold with false clues and unexpected twists. The circularity of time travel becomes the perfect metaphor to depict the cycles of toxic relationships and familial abuse and show how the participants, no matter how unwilling, are often too helpless and afraid to break the cycle. All the members involved in the time loop form an interconnected family tree, linked to each other by a distinct *lack* of love, often growing up to murder those with whom they share blood relations. In fact, the show barely dwells on wholesome and loving relationships, suggesting that while cycles of abuse are endlessly repeated in a loop, relationships based on mutual trust cannot survive in such a world.

Jonas and Martha seem to share an inexplicable bond, yet like Romeo and Juliet, can never be united. Instead, they are forced to confront the fact that they themselves are the glitch in the matrix, that their love is impossible and never meant to be. So in a moment of selflessness, Jonas and Martha travel to the "origin world" (where the time travel was invented and must be unmade) to stop a car crash and prevent the family of Tannhaus (the fictional scientist who creates a time machine and accidentally opens a portal inside the caves) from falling apart. Once the mission is complete, they dissolve into dust, holding hands, as all the other characters who were born as a product of time travel slowly fade away.

In the show's epilogue, once the timelines have been unmade, we get a glimpse of some of the characters (who were related to the family tree but not born *directly* as a result of someone time-traveling) sharing a toast, seemingly free of malice and manipulation, a picture of what wholesome relationships can be like when people have learned to let go at the right time.

I found the end of *Dark* satisfying and immensely sad. Having binge-watched three seasons in a span of a week and a half, and becoming deeply invested in the characters, it felt strange to let go, to realize there isn't a new season to look forward to. Stories, I suppose, are only meaningful if they have a beginning, middle and end (though not necessarily in that order) and needlessly prolonging the inevitable can only result in a sort of tedious mediocrity or even destroy what gave it meaning in the first place (season 8 of *Game of Thrones*, anyone?).

Moreover, by letting go of each other, Jonas and Martha do not just die, but stop existing, as though they were never real, as though their love was nothing more than a dream. It made me re-evaluate my relationship with someone I was deeply in love with for almost two years, who it transpired, did not care about me at all, whose words destroyed my self-worth and self-image to the point I'd wake up in the middle of the night with a panic attack and cry profusely. With my classes suspended, I had more free time on my schedule than ever, only to be fired out of the blue by the company I'd worked at for the last three years, leaving me with no source of income. I haven't seen some of my closest friends in five months, and with my university life so abruptly concluded, I wonder if we'll ever be as close anymore.

The loneliness brought about by the pandemic gave me a lot of time to consider past relationships and former career dreams, to face the grief that comes from being forced to let go, *against* your will, of old loves, habits, beliefs. It taught me that by trying to hold onto things that we know we'll inevitably lose (failing friendships, a soul-sucking job, a career path that curves on itself to lead only to dead ends) we risk making it worse, we risk destroying it utterly.

The ultimate plot-twist in the narrative of *Dark* is that time travel isn't a product of technological evolution but a bootstrap paradox that sustains itself by the characters' inability to let go of each other and a desire to change their own past. If there's a final lesson to it, it's this: that letting go of what you love is the most selfless act there is.

The only way out of Ariadne's labyrinth, is to let go, even if it means losing something precious forever and starting again, anew.

Eternally Controversial: Doom Eternal and its place in a controversial franchise

BY B. NARR

"Creative works don't exist in a vacuum, and every story carries subtext and social implications with it, whether those are put there purposefully or not. Not every story needs to have a moral—far from it—and no creative work is without flaws, but creators always need to be aware of what our works will say once they've been released out into the wild blue yonder of the public. We need to know what social context we're releasing it into. We need to know whose rhetoric we're borrowing."

In the world of first-person shooters, *Doom* is about as iconic as it gets— and for good reason. With its fast-paced fights, hulking weapons, unsettling monsters, realistic gore, and a stoic (yet sassy) main character, it has all the makings of a great time for those who like their games chock-full of ripping and tearing.

The most current addition to the series, *Doom Eternal* (*id Software and Bethesda Softworks*, 2020), is no exception. The sequel to *Doom* (2016), and the fifth main game in the Doom series, has all the hallmarks of a Doom game. You walk through an extravagantly rendered hellscape as the Doom Slayer, a killer soundtrack in your wake, while you try to make your way through frantic battles, puzzles, and—my personal favorite—battle puzzles. It might even be more over-the-top than the past games, but the gameplay principles are the same as ever: keep an eye out for ammo drops and keep moving. While there's the occasional cutscene, the story is largely embedded into the world itself. You pick up pieces of written lore or else run into what is essentially flavor text from a holographic spokesperson for the bad guys, the UAC (Union Aerospace Corporation), a fictional multi-planetary conglomerate.

That's where things got dicey.

Phrases like "Your suffering continues to inspire us!" and "No one is born a sinner. You have to work hard to achieve success!" are delivered in a chipper, let's-focus-on-company-synergy voice every time you pass one of the hologram projectors. (And there are quite a few hologram projectors.) The UAC spokesperson's dialogue is on-brand for the game, no doubt. Tongue-in-cheek dark humor is a cornerstone of the *Doom* franchise.

Unfortunately, she also introduces a phrase that has been the source of controversy since the game's demo release in 2018. She asks everyone to refer to the demons as "mortally challenged," since "demon can be an offensive term." For those who missed it, gaming writer Astrid Johnson wrote a whole piece on why this was an unsavory choice of words when the demo was released. The term was only said once in the demo, but now that the game is out, players can see that "mortally challenged" pops up a *lot*, via the UAC spokesperson's dialogue and pieces of lore written by the good guys—it's definitely not just a one-off joke.

But why, in a game full of violence and death, is that the thing that stood out to a lot of players?

Let's go back to 1993, where all of this started.

After the success of *Wolfenstein 3D* (1992), the tiny team at id Software decided to create something a little different: one of the first truly 3d first-person shooters. It would be fast, it would be bloody, and it would be self-published via shareware (meaning anyone could download it). They had no idea the splash their space-marine-blasting-his-way-through-literal-hell would make in the video game industry.

Once you get past the basic premise of carving through demons, the story tends to slide into the background in the early games, probably because story always came second to gameplay and graphics at id Software. (In fact, one of the original team members who wanted to take *Doom* in a more story-driven direction was stopped at every turn, and eventually replaced.) But id Software didn't need to have a complex story to cause controversy in the 90s. Their visuals took care of that.

Doom's violence and satanic imagery, complete with level names like *Knee-Deep in the Dead*, appalled parents and pearl-clutchers alike. People started to blame real-life violence on it, even going so far as to say that it taught kids how to kill. The game, along with its fellow blood-gusher Mortal Kombat, was the subject of a 1993 congressional hearing on video game violence. It was specifically mentioned as one of the games played by the perpetrators of the Columbine Massacre in 1999.

None of that stopped *Doom* from being one of the most acclaimed first-person shooters of all time.

In fact, the controversy fueled them. Every successive game was gorier—with the help of continuously better graphics—and every game continued to garner some level of criticism along with their accolades, but none received the virulent reaction that the first *Doom* got. "Brutal" was a common compliment in reviews. The pentagrams weren't shocking. We expected blood and guts from *Doom*. By *Doom III*'s release in 2004, the franchise was no longer a subject of major controversy.

Over a decade later, id Software released a reboot. It still had the same basic premise, but with a more complex storyline expected from modern games. That's when we finally have enough narrative material to see a running theme that's not just game mechanics.

The original *Doom*'s story could be seen as a critique of the military-industrial complex. The main character is a marine sent to a Mars outpost as punishment for refusing to kill civilians, who, due to the greed and hubris of a megacorporation, is forced to fight his way through hordes of interdimensional demons. It brings to mind the WWI Marine Major General Smedley Butler's take on his role in war: "I was a racketeer; a gangster for capitalism." As the Doom Slayer, we play someone who has refused to be that, someone who is fighting the very machine that once employed him. That fact hasn't changed over the course of the franchise. (There *has* been a lot of story added, but don't worry, no major spoilers for the new stuff here.)

What's more is that the unnamed marine in *Doom* is canonically the descendant of William Blazkowicz, the Jewish Army Captain who's been fighting Nazis in *Wolfenstein*, also a product of id Software and Bethesda (and a lot of other companies), since 1981. It's difficult to imagine that a company that made both of those games would purposefully cater to a small subset of right-wing reactionaries, as Astrid Johnson pointed out in her article on the issue. However, it's *not* difficult to imagine that id Software inadvertently parroted them in an attempt to maintain their edgy, controversial status.

Frankly, the "mortally challenged" jokes feel like a hackneyed attempt to revive the controversy that *Doom* used to feed on. No longer are gamers shocked by video game violence. No longer are there fleets of those pearl-clutching parents condemning the satanic imagery being shoved into their children's eyeballs. Those folks have found other things to focus on, and—intentionally or not—*Doom* has swiveled to the side of the pearl-clutchers and vaulted past them straight into conservative rhetoric. Is this supposed to shock and appall us, the players? Were the gore and the demons not meant *for* us in the first place? Or do the developers of *Doom Eternal* think, as so many game developers still seem to, that their audience solely consists of stereotypical white cishet right-wing dudes who spend their free time ranting about "SJWs" on YouTube?

I'm not the first person to point out that the video game community is a diverse one, nor am I the first person to point out that this extends to games like *Doom*, too. We like killing demons as much as anyone else, but when there are a series of casual digs at other folks' humanity, sometimes even our own humanity, it's hard to ignore. Ignoring it, in fact, means accepting it—accepting that, while we're allowed to play this game, there are people who equate us and our loved ones to the monsters, not the hero.

Creative works don't exist in a vacuum, and every story carries subtext and social implications with it, whether those are put there purposefully or not. Not every story needs to have a moral—far from it—and no creative work is without flaws, but creators always need to be aware of what our works will say once they've been released out into the wild blue yonder of the public. We need to know what social context we're releasing it into. We need to know whose rhetoric we're borrowing.

We need to know what ammo we're dropping, and who might pick it up.

Remnant: From the Ashes is a Metaphor for Climate Change: Reconciling Colonialism, Hyperconsumerism, and the Fun of Fighting Badass Monsters

BY COREY J. WHITE

The hub world of *Remnant: From the Ashes* (*RFTA, Perfect World Entertainment/Gunfire Games*, 2019) is one dominated by plant life. Gargantuan trees loom over the starting city and grow in and through buildings, weird fungal growths litter the environment, and everywhere you go humanoid motile trees are trying to cut you to pieces, skewer you with arrows, or charge toward you aflame with suicidal/homicidal resolve. Collectively these trees are The Root, the game's major threat.

In this time of major ecological crisis, it's hard not to read an eco-political message into a game in which the trees themselves are rising up against man, laying waste to the symbols of civilization and industry. Maybe these representatives of nature are trying to wipe out humanity in retribution for the damage our actions have wrought on the world. It's us or them, and at the start of the game, they're winning.

Colony Collapse

After fighting through a veritable forest of vengeful trees and killing vicious bosses on Earth, you will find yourself at a gateway to other worlds. The first world you reach is called Rhom. According to the lore, the people of Rhom are the only ones to have defeated The Root, but at the cost of their civilization. The skeletal remains of buildings litter the land, their exposed metal frames standing strong against the desert winds even as the cement erodes. The locals don't dwell in these ruins—instead, they've constructed new towns, adobe houses decorated with pottery and bones, lit braziers, simple furniture, and tools. The people are accompanied by domesticated dogs and defend their homes with a ferocity unmatched even by The Root—it's no wonder they came out on top.

Indeed, after being greeted by a herald, your next encounter on Rhom will be a violent one. These people have seen what happens when armed outsiders come into their midst, and they will do anything to protect their way of life. Like all colonizers though, you arrive with superior firepower, strolling through the interplanetary portal with high-powered rifles, submachine guns, and war hammers made from motorcycle engines (not to mention the special power known as "being the player character").

First, you'll kill all the townsfolk and their loyal dogs, and then you'll ransack their homes, smashing everything in sight for the scrap you use as currency. What might these pots contain? Who cares, smash 'em for scrap! What is the cultural significance of these urns? Who cares, smash 'em for scrap! What might these alters laden with bones tell us about the spiritual beliefs of these people? Who cares, smash it all!

It's a story as old as empire—people driven by their need for glory travel to distant lands, kill or enslave the people living there because they are somehow *less than*, destroy the symbols of their culture, steal their valuables, and return home feeling like champions and great explorers. (But you can't "discover" a place where people are already living. It doesn't work like that.)

The Consequences of Colonialism

And whilst the age of empires (no, not *that* Age of Empires) might have come to an end, we still live within its shadow. All around the real-life world, academics and activists of various stripes are grappling with the many consequences of colonialism. For obvious reasons though, governments and other institutions can be hostile to post-colonial points of view that might force them to confront their actions and the damage wrought in their names.

It's refreshing to see a game not only grapple with the issues of colonialism, but to also put the player in the role of the genocider, to force us to come to grips with our own complicity in these systems of slavery, murder, and control. (My tongue is firmly in my cheek here. Not only does the game offer no commentary on your imperialist actions, you are, of course, rewarded with XP and currency for your wanton destruction of the locals, their belongings, and their way of life.)

Gameplay: Surviving the Post-Apocalypse

But what does this have to do with our current ecological crisis? It's exactly these extractavist colonial ideologies that feed into the hyperconsumerism of today. Whilst the planet itself seems to be telling us that there are limits to what damage it can sustain whilst staying within liveable limits for us and the many other species that had adapted and survived to pre-industrial times, we have labored for centuries now under the myth that there is always more *just over there*. There is always more land for crops, more animals for food, more gold, more workers (both willing and un)—all we need to do is get in a boat and travel over the horizon until we find a new place to destroy and a new people to subjugate. Similarly, if we're worried about where we're going to dump all of the mountains of trash we create, we can simply put it on a boat to Asia somewhere, and let them worry about it.

Don't think about the enslaved people mining precious metals for your next smartphone, or the enslaved people working to ensure you have chocolate, almonds, and countless other products. If we're worried about the damage being done to the environment by our consumption, we can find sustainable ways to consume . . . because heaven forbid it's that relationship to consumption that we begin to question. The hub world of *RFTA* might be desolate and dilapidated, but as long as there are other worlds populated by people whose personhood we are unwilling (or unable) to respect, then we will find plenty of currency and crafting materials to propel us forward on our colonialist mission.

I've spent these words talking about subtexts that probably weren't intended to be in the game. But that's the great thing about Soulslike games and their penchant for a more minimalist storytelling style—it gives the player space to read between the lines—and I wouldn't have dived so deep on the game if it hadn't gotten its hooks into me. Since I first played Dark Souls I've wanted a Soulslike with continuous (online) co-op, and *RFTA* has given me exactly what I wanted, spread across multiple worlds and tied together with a sci-fi story I can't help but get caught up in.

Remnant: From the Ashes is well worth playing. But as you play through this game about an interdimensional threat to all life, and the brave warriors who are prepared to put a stop to it, ask yourself, which one of those describes the plants, and which describes the people? Maybe, just maybe it's not the plants that are the real threat.

Double Visions: Two Mysteries for Today's World: Reading Frankie Y. Bailey and Claire O'Dell's all-too-near futures

BY JAMILEH JEMISON

"...here is a chance to revel in an America with women of color and queer leaders and heroines—a lovely, audacious hope."

So...how are you doing with this pandemic thing? Did this new-to-humans disease, spreading like wildfire, shutting down nations, economies, and maybe civilizations make you feel like you woke up as a character in one of the spec-fic books on your TBR? Anybody? Just me? Or maybe the questions about what life will look like after this—whenever that is—have got you writing existentialist plague diaries in your head, or dusting off your 'new civil war' letters from when it was just a meme.

If you find it comforting that some authors have wondered about this very moment before, *and* you find a mystery diverting, I've got two amazing authors and four books of their alternate-universe United States for you to explore (and maybe shape your revolution manifesto) while you are 'social distancing.'

Here are two writers and two series, each two books deep, with new perspectives on our near future.

Frankie Y. Bailey writes such tight near fiction timelines that her two Hannah McCabe novels are now near-history, though set only months ago. *The Red Queen Dies* (*Minotaur Books,* 2013) looked ahead to an alternate-universe summer 2019 in Albany, NY where biracial police detective Hannah McCabe snags an unwieldy case that might be a serial killer, or just someone trying to look like one? The plot taps unique elements of Albany's history with nods to Lewis Carroll, Sir Arthur Conan Doyle, and Houdini, as Hannah and her partner try to find a clear motive and the culprit.

Hannah's world largely resembles our own: thick with the political tensions we walked into IRL; featuring technology and transportation options that could be next-generation releases (and maybe not welcome ones); and a miasma that waxes and wanes in the air, sickening her partner and making summer storms a reason to stay locked up indoors (sound a bit familiar?).

Book two of the Detective Hannah McCabe series *What The Fly Saw* followed in 2015 and is set in January 2020 (a month we're all giving a retrospective side-eye) and may cause a bit of *déjà vu*. A catastrophic event abroad requires mandatory evacuation of foreigners and impacts Hannah's life as she is trying to solve a twisty murder with too many false leads. This plot reveals more about Hannah's unique family, a nice break from 'lone wolf' detective characters, and probes society's current mode of unquestioningly adopting new technologies.

If you chose to read all these books in the order discussed here, the Sir Arthur Conan Doyle nods in *Queen* and the scientific themes of *Fly* cue up perfectly with Claire O'Dell's *Janet Watson Chronicles*.

A Study In Honor (*Harper Voyager*, 2018) follows Dr. Janet Watson, former army surgeon, and Ms. Sara Holmes (yes that kind of Holmes and Watson) live in an America some years further into our future. Trump is a former president. There was indeed a New Civil War and Dr. Watson is returning home to Washington, DC after her convalescence, determined to restart her life after a combat injury. Fate and an old friend introduce her to the enigmatic Holmes, who is looking for a tolerant roommate.

The tip of the deerstalker to Sir Arthur Conan Doyle is intentional. There are familiar gracenotes of the original characters and relationships to please avid fans, but this recast centers black women as the famous duo, a broad spectrum of POC including out proud queer POC, and the political and technological context of a troubled near-future America. It's a familiar gateway to some great questions about where America is going.

The book is both origin story and first case for this iteration of Watson and Holmes. Their relationship remains a central and essential element to the storytelling, and they soon find a consuming case intriguing enough for Holmes but haunting for Janet as she gets reacquainted with her city and adjusts to her eccentric roommate and life after war. *The Hound of Justice* (2019) is a true sequel. It picks up a few months after the end of *Honor* and finds the pair in pursuit of a diabolically resilient villain. The plot escalates rapidly to an intense case in which Holmes and Watson must both operate at the peak of their very different skills, while trying to understand and hold onto a friendship under strain.

These aren't cozy mysteries, but they aren't grisly procedurals either. I have a fondness for both and an insatiable appetite for Sherlock adaptations, but what I truly love about these novels, and the reason I reread them, is their humanity. Here are professional women, all unpartnered for various reasons, doing their interesting jobs, which drive the plot, while figuring out how to care for their aging parents, feeling nervous about a potential love interest, coming to terms with a changed body. The familiarity of these mundane challenges, makes me trust the characters and believe the AU.

Four novels, two writers, two subtly-updated future Americas so well synchronized, they are practically a continuum. Hannah McCabe solves engaging whodunnits, while Watson and Holmes tangle with the institutions and architects of these nascent dystopias. The similarities between these AUs and our lives may discomfit you, but take heart, mysteries always end with a solution.

And if you've been disappointed with our political choices lately, here's a chance to revel in an America with women of color and queer leaders and heroines—a lovely, audacious hope.

In 21st-Century America, Who Gets to be Magic?: The Magicians and Representation

BY JAMILEH JEMISON

We are no longer living in the stale idyll of 'classic' 1950s fantasy, nodding along that whiteness and the patriarchy are anointed norms. Yet, The Magicians unconsciously tells us that in 21st-century America only straight, white people get to have magic.

The Magicians (2015–2020) is a slick, snarky, campy fantasy series based on the novel of the same name by Lev Grossman. It ran five seasons on SyFy from Dec 2015 to Apr 1, 2020. The first four seasons are on Netflix where I drank them down like an icy, non-diet, soda on a hot summer's day; so satisfying, so many empty calories.

It's present-day New York City. The theory of magic is: it exists, but you wouldn't know it unless you have the talent, which you learn at a school of magic, or from a hedge. In this universe, people who use magic are called (logically) magicians, rather than witch/wizard/mage etc., and the storytelling revolves around eight friends—four men, four women, only one person of color, only one white, gay man—and their love and loyalty-driven misadventures.

The charm of the show for me was its humor: ludicrous overcrowding of fantasy tropes, irreverent treatment of literature's early magical forerunners, talking rabbits. And I loved it's commitment to a consistent visual language.

The visuals aren't award-worthy, but they're evocative and demonstrate that someone made careful choices about how the show should look and what each look should mean. And that's where it gets uncomfortable because the creative team's careful choices flaunt rather outdated ideas about who gets to be magical. Please note this discussion contains some non-specific spoilers.

My brother used to joke that NBC stood for 'No Black Characters.' The first two seasons of *The Magicians* are remarkably thin on people of color. Penny is Indian and the only POC in the core group of characters. The first black man to show up has longevity on the show but is openly described as a functional alcoholic and is often the dupe.

Someone must have noticed and said something because from season three onward there are black *men* everywhere, two are featured as love interests for white core characters and one bangs a blonde woman in a closet (sexual exoticization anyone?) as some background oddness to a tense showdown. There are a few black women on the show with a few lines each, but the one with the largest role is a vehicle for catharsis for one of the four white female core characters. At least she got a multi-season arc? Asian women appear in two episodes. All play strong magicians but have maybe thirty lines between the three of them, including a character who does not speak English. Asian men, aside from Penny also get episodes, both men are also strong magicians, but one has a single line then is dead in the next scene, the other has maybe ten lines and his arc is over in the next scene.

Latinx? Who? Apparently there aren't any Latinx people in this 21st-century AU NYC, and none of them have magic, nor are the gods or magical ideas of Spanish-speaking heritage mentioned in a show that frequently name-checks the obscure language a spell is written in. *sigh* The most depressing stereotype on the show (because it gets so much screen time) is the openly alcoholic, sexually inappropriate, chronically angry, exiled Russian man. Holy caricatures, Batman!

On the sexuality front, there is a beautiful, unfaltering, fluid friendship between the one gay character (TOGC) and his female best friend. There is a beautiful, undefined, fluid family unit of TOGC, the nominal protagonist (a whiny, straight white male), his wife, and their child. There's a matter of fact, no labels, just fun threesome, all of which gave me hope for a really present-tense, gender-is-over, all-relationships-under-the-rainbow culture percolating in the background of the high (melo)drama.

But no such luck. A lot of plot work is done to make sure there are equal numbers of men and women in the core group at all times, setting a subtle but heavy 'presumptive heterosexuality' vibe. There are multiple plots that feature or hinge on marriage, even TOGC gets married to a woman, and there are at least three pregnancies. Other openly gay characters are all men who are introduced solely as love interests for TOGC and then disappear. Women kiss but it's voyeuristic and eroticized. And there are no trans people.

That all leaves a whiff of stale apple pie and sweaty baseball uniforms. But then there's a predatory pedophile, a monster that is a gigantic walking metaphor for repressed desire and shame, and a rape—but don't worry they flashed a rape crisis hotline on the screen before the credits. Again, *sigh*

Why does this matter? If you're even a bit interested in *The Magicians* you may have read some or all of Ben Aaronovitch, Dante Alighieri, Ilona Andrews, Emma Bull, Jim Butcher, Susanna Clarke, Deborah Harkness, Kim Harrison, CS Lewis, Rob Thurman.

These authors taught me every creature, beast, magical race, cultural pantheon, portal/veil, magical object, and supernatural etiquette one needs to know to feel like *The Magicians* is a long-form inside joke on 'theories of magic in fantasy novels' written just for you. I think this is why *The Magicians* is so popular—it feels like a fantasy written for grown-ups. It's for the generation that grew up reading fantasy and loving it. *The Magicians* takes tropes and plays with them. Seeing this series take on what I've accidentally been studying through my book choices, made me feel seen, and like I was part of a discourse.

Except. Except, I (a black woman) am hardly on the screen. Does that mean black women don't have magic? Or, as it plays out, the purpose of a black woman's magic is to bring about the self-actualization of a white woman? What about my friends who are trans? Who are lesbians? Who are proudly from Mexico, Columbia, Peru, Vietnam? Why aren't they in the conversation? Why can't they have magic?

It only takes a few SFF series to get a good sense of the mainstays of Western imagination around magic, gods, and an encyclopedic menagerie of magical beings. It's rare to see a new magical species or plot twist, so the fun is viewing these canonical ideas through new eyes.

When those new eyes try to tell me with a straight face that there are dragons, gods, and vodyanoi living in New York City, but there are only five Asian people in their entire magical multiverse, I get confused. Why can you imagine and celebrate such diversity in invisible realms of supernatural power, but not even acknowledge the extant diversity in the world where you have set your tale?

We are no longer living in the stale idyll of 'classic' 1950s fantasy, nodding along that whiteness and the patriarchy are anointed norms. Yet, *The Magicians* unconsciously tells us that in 21st-century America only straight, white people get to have magic. I call that a failure of imagination.

Goblin Slayer and the Importance of Hope in Grimdark Fantasy: In a world of darkness and suffering, He Does Not Let Anyone Roll The Dice

BY KYLE TAM

Goblin Slayer, his party, and his allies will not allow their narratives to be controlled by the suffering and pain they have experienced. Instead, they work together to bring active and positive change to the world, to create a place where the trauma they have experienced is no longer necessary.

TW: sexual violence, rape, trauma, death.

The word *grimdark* often conjures up images of despair, of universes where no matter what you do, nothing will ever be enough. Violence, assault, and the ensuing trauma are considered par for the course, and it is often an excuse to portray utter bleakness with nary a chance for change. *Goblin Slayer* (*Yen Press*, 2016), a light novel series by Kumo Kagyu, certainly begins in the same manner. Of the three available mediums to engage with *Goblin Slayer*, the light novels, as translated by Yen Press, have both the most tact and most respect for victims, which is why they're the medium being discussed here.

Before diving into *Goblin Slayer*, however, there is one important thing that must be addressed. Much of *Goblin Slayer's* premise is predicated not only on violence but typically sexual violence; it is used to show the depravity of the goblins. Could this story have been written without it? Yes, absolutely.

Sexual violence is never a necessity in any work, and although there is a history of it in Japanese *grimdark* works, such as popular mangas Berserk by Kentaro Miura (*Dark Horse Comics,* 1989-Present) or Gantz by Hiroya Oku (*Dark Horse Comics,* 2007), it is an artifact of an era that relished in depicting brutality towards women. Even though there is much to be commended in what *Goblin Slayer* does to uplift survivors, the books are still not an easy read due to their graphic depictions of assault.

With that being said, most depictions of sexual violence in the novels provide us with the *aftermath* rather than the act. Where there is actively described violence, it is still remarkably bloody, but merely alludes to a sexually violent act that is to occur. This is not the case in the anime and manga, which often seem to relish in on-screen depictions of active violence and brutalization of victims; the anime was even marketed in the West as a standard swords & sorcery adventure and mistakenly given the label of PG—appropriate for children.

In the first entry of this twelve-volume series, the demon king and his army are approaching from all sides, there are monsters scattered all over the continent, and goblins, the underlings of the demon king and the main series antagonists, regularly terrorize and destroy villages. The very first chapter of the novels even begins with a goblin ambush that leaves two adventurers dead, one sexually assaulted, and another left haunted by the ordeal. *Goblin Slayer*, however, differs from its contemporaries in that it does not barrage you with a message of utter nihilism. Instead, it depicts a world of blossoming hope where survivors band together and provide a catalyst for change, in order to protect others from suffering the same ordeal.

In the youth of the nameless, titular Goblin Slayer—simply referred to as Goblin Slayer in the series—witnesses the rape and murder of his sister and the destruction of his village at the hand of goblins, an event that is alluded to, but not described in the detail some authors may have relished in. When we meet him, he is obsessed with killing goblins, perpetually patrolling or preparing, and largely considered bizarre by his guildmates.

However, the catalyst for Goblin Slayer's character growth throughout the series is not his unstoppable quest for vengeance, but by the eventual support and friendship, he gains in both his newly found adventuring party and a wider network of allies. The Goblin Slayer learns to trust others, to include them in his plans, and to aid them in theirs, rather than working by himself. He chooses to take on the novice Priestess, a traumatized adventurer from Chapter One, because he is in need of a healer and, as we learn later on, to help her overcome the pain he once had to face alone.

We even find that his work in eradicating goblins and working with his fellow man has active, tangible benefits. In his very first mission, Goblin Slayer protected a small village and little girl from harm. That little girl grows up to become a Chosen Hero, destined to slay the demon king and save the world, not broken and burdened but with hope coming out of every pore. At no point is trauma considered wholly definitive in his journey, and at no point is it considered a good force for his character development. Instead, the Goblin Slayer is fighting evil, trying to prevent the unhappiness of his experience from happening to anyone ever again.

The theme of survivors moving forward with the support of others is a constant thread throughout the series, reinforced by characters such as Sword Maiden and Noble Fencer. Sword Maiden is an A-Rank adventurer, the highest ranking that any adventurer can achieve. In her first adventure, however, she was assaulted and blinded by a band of goblins and eventually escaped. It is not something she discusses except with trusted confidantes, as she is afraid of ridicule and dismissiveness, mortified that even with all her strength and prowess, it happened to her; she lives with night terrors, with the very real fear of facing goblins once again.

But her tragic past is never used to diminish her, and she is never dismissed by our protagonists or by the narrative. She provides support where she can through the use of magic or political clout, and by speaking with Goblin Slayer about their shared pain, she is able to find some measure of comfort. He promises her he will slay the goblins in her dreams, and she is finally able to have a good night's rest.

Then there is Noble Fencer; she is a haughty and overconfident adventurer on her first journey, whose character arc is one of burning vengeance. Goblin Slayer's party is tasked with retrieving her. They find her half-dead, her party wiped out by goblins, and it is Goblin Slayer's companion Priestess who recognizes that if they do not take her with them to confront her literal demons she may break entirely. So Noble Fencer joins the party on their quest to eradicate the goblins that used and abused her, and ultimately realizes that life as an adventurer is not for her.

She is never shamed for choosing to walk away and comes back into the narrative a few volumes later as a character known as the Female Merchant Leader. In this capacity, she uses her influence and financial capability to campaign for and fund novice adventurer training, something that would have a real benefit for those who were in the position she was in. It is the first real institutional reform that we see being enacted in the novels properly.

What ties these three together is that they have chosen to help others in spite of the very real pain that they have endured. It would be easy for them to turn their backs, to have nothing to do with anything and work in their own self-interests, but they all recognize the horrible things that happened to others as well and take active steps to create a better world. At the same time, there is never any blame put on survivors of goblin attacks, and there is never any shame for continuing on with one's life afterward. Villages still celebrate festivals, weddings still take place, and there is still happiness and kindness in the world. There is pain and suffering throughout, but even so, life goes on, and rather than mocking this jubilation as ill-intentioned or wasteful in a world with misery on all sides, efforts are taken to protect this way of life.

Alexandra Rowland once described the antithesis of *grimdark* as *hopepunk*, where the prevailing message of a piece of media is to keep fighting and hold on to hope, and the *hopepunk* aesthetic describes *Goblin Slayer* perfectly. It is a world of bleak misery, where human lives are decided at the whims of the god's dice, which is why the declaration that He Will Not Let Anyone Roll The Dice which adorns every cover is so important.

Goblin Slayer, his party, and his allies will not allow their narratives to be controlled by the suffering and pain they have experienced. Instead, they work together to bring active and positive change to the world, to create a place where the trauma they have experienced is no longer necessary. *Goblin Slayer's* central concept is that trauma and suffering may be *formative*, enough to shape one's purpose, but it does not have to be *definitive*.

Goblin Slayer isn't the kind of story that begins with suffering and ends with suffering, where characters are haphazardly left to nurse their wounds and are corrupted by their agony. It is a story of redemption, of finding the light at the end of the tunnel, of facing the darkness in the world and coming out stronger – not by magic and power, but through trust, care, and support. In a medium often defined by the trauma conga line characters are subjected to without any hint of reprieve, *Goblin Slayer* demonstrates that there is always hope so long as we work together and support one another, that trauma does not have to define you, and that it is crucial to support and believe survivors.

Grunge, Metal, and AP Chemistry: Review of Rosebud Ben-Oni's 20 Atomic Sonnets

BY LESLIE ARCHIBALD

"For me chemistry represented an indefinite cloud of future potentialities which enveloped my life... I'd watch the buds swell in spring, the mica glint in the granite, my own ands, and I would say to myself: I will understand this, too, I will understand everything." — Primo Levi

I love sonnets. I also hate them. Sonnets, done well, can be small explosions of inspiration and emotion. If the rhyme is off even slightly or seems forced, they feel trite and mechanical. I wanted to review this collection of sonnets because I wanted to fall in love. I wanted to fall in love with the sonnet again and I did.

In the collection 20 *Atomic Sonnets* (*Black Warrior Review*, 2020) by award-winning poet Rosebud Ben-Oni, the unique structure coupled with the author's use of slant and embedded rhyme creates the sonnet aesthetic without overpowering the text. In some sonnets, the poem becomes so much about the form that the words are lost in structure. Here, the form emphasizes changes in composition and creates a surprising reading experience.

Ben-Oni uses elements from the periodic table to explore the duality of science and nature found within each. She explores the reactions and interactions of the elements by personifying them through memorable images and emotive language. Specifically, "77Ir :: *r u dense?* {I'm the *Baddest* Kiss}," The element, Iridium, known to be a dense rigid metal, is projected as a strong, feminine force who seems to run her own show.

Ben-Oni pays homage to nineties metal poets by relating certain elements to groups like Nirvana, STP, and Bon Jovi. I found these references relatable and thoughtful. Metal bands tend to be misunderstood and complicated much like the elements on the periodic table. In the poem, "112Cn :: Come as You Are {Un Un Bi Ummmmm}," which refers to the grunge band Nirvana, she chooses copernicium which is radioactive and unstable, lasting only "half a minute." A poignant reference to the short life of frontman Kurt Cobain.

Later poems move the reader into the electric dance music (EDM) of a rave and the lack of human intimacy that comes with it. The morose sonnet, "14SI :: {ok!} Computer" is set in a time where AI pushes humanity into darkness (or perhaps humanity creates their own darkness).

I asked the author why she chose to write sonnets about elements on a periodic table and her answer was simple. She had spent so much time with them in AP Chemistry they became familiar. "I began coming up with my own "stories" about each element, giving them personalities, attitudes, desires, and such, and included a note or two for these stories on the back of the flashcards," She said. Since last year was the 150th birthday of the periodic table it seemed the right time to build on the, in her words, "seeds of those original ideas."

Curiously, Ben-Oni is not the first to dive into the periodic table in poetry form. Maggie Schold created a periodic table of poetry in 1998 (still accessible via Internet Archive) and several online poetry collectives created a periodic table of haiku, such as this one circa 2001. Even fiction has used this device, as in Primo Levi's short story collection, *The Periodic Table* (Levi is quoted in the beginning of this collection). Just last year, speculative poet Mary Soon Lee published *Elemental Haiku,* another collection of periodic poetry.

If you are like me and haven't seen a periodic table since the ninth grade (Physical Science wasn't required in my high school and Biology was my science of choice in college), don't let that keep you from reading this collection. The collection is annotated, and the annotations feel as poetic as the sonnets themselves. I found the annotations to be helpful to understand the elements and the correlations with our own actions which is what I feel this collection was about. Understanding.

I also asked the author about distribution during the unique circumstances that we are living in today. "I wanted to make 20 *Atomic Sonnets* free & available online, as to reach as many people as possible in the time of this pandemic," She said. When she told me her plans, I once again thought of the Silicon sonnet "Computer" and how dependent we are on computers during this pandemic. The screen of a computer is now our primary vessel for interacting with others. The pandemic has isolated us indoors where, as the sonnet says, the sun may as well have "burned out."

20 *Atomic Sonnets* is available online now as a special gift from the author during this pandemic. Get your free copy here.

About the Author

Rosebud Ben-Oni is the winner of the 2019 Alice James Award for *If This Is the Age We End Discovery*, forthcoming in 2021, and the author of *turn around, BRXGHT XYXS* (Get Fresh Books, 2019). She is a recipient of fellowships from the New York Foundation for the Arts (NYFA) and CantoMundo. Her work appears in *POETRY, The American Poetry Review, POETS.org, The Poetry Review* (UK), *Tin House, Guernica, Black Warrior Review, Prairie Schooner, Electric Literature, TriQuarterly, Hayden's Ferry Review*, among others. Her poem "Poet Wrestling with Angels in the Dark" was commissioned by the National September 11 Memorial & Museum in New York City and published by *The Kenyon Review Online*. She writes for *The Kenyon Review* blog, and recently edited a special chemistry poetry portfolio for *Pleiades*. Find her at 7TrainLove.org.

On Watching Every Episode of Hellier in
One Week: Kentucky goblins, UFO
sightings, and high strangeness in the heart
of Appalachia

BY CASSANDRA ROSE CLARKE

"UFO stories were, I realized, the same as fairy stories, only filtered through the language of the 20th century: flying saucers and unimaginable science and shadowy Feds in low-brimmed hats."

Every ten years or so I go through a phase wherein I spend a lot of time thinking about UFOs.

It was the late 90s, and I was in junior high. I listened to the *X-Files* soundtrack and bought jewelry with wide-eyed aliens on it and kept an inflatable plastic alien in my room, which was decorated with glow-in-the-dark plastic stars and Mulder's *I want to believe* poster.

Ten years later, after I finished graduate school and was teaching high school in a very small Texas town currently only known to the rest of the world because a lady who lived there claimed she had a chupacabra head in her freezer, I found myself watching reality TV alien investigation documentaries on a regular basis, which lead to a tumble-dive into your basic bitch UFO conspiracy theories. For example, I read *Communion*. I did some minor stargazing. Looked up Area 51 on Google Earth.

As obsessions tend to do, UFOs found their way into my fiction. The year I thought constantly about aliens and men in black and hidden underground government bases was also the year I made my first pro sale, to *Strange*

Horizons: "The Space Between Stars," a story about Area 51 and Las Vegas existing in the same desert. That summer, I attended Clarion West, and I wrote another story, never published, called "Thirty-Nine Miles to Dreamland". This one was about an observation I made, sometime between watching a scientist dismiss cattle mutilations on Hulu and watching the living cows graze behind my backyard: that UFO stories and all their related ephemera, known to nerds like me by the rather poetic name of high strangeness, share the same DNA as fairy stories.

Not fairy *tales*, but stories *about* fairies. The stories that warn against stepping into a circle of mushrooms, of passing into the realm of Faerie and losing decades of your life. The stories of meeting the Devil, a man dressed in black, at a crossroads to sell your soul for music. The stories of strange small creatures who steal your keys unless you leave a bowl of milk in a window.

UFO stories were, I realized, the same as fairy stories, only filtered through the language of the 20th century: flying saucers and unimaginable science and shadowy Feds in low-brimmed hats. It struck me at the time as profound, an insight into something about the stories we tell each other, the layers of truth we might find if we peel back the skin of fiction and get to its heart.

This was all ten years ago, like I said. In 2010. Which meant the decade has circled around again, and UFOs have to come back into my life.

This is probably why I wound up watching *Hellier*.

Hellier is a documentary series on Amazon Prime about a team of paranormal researchers investigating a claim by a Kentucky doctor that his family is being terrorized by aliens that more or less look like the inflatable doll I had when I was thirteen. Except it's not really about that.

I watched the first season of *Hellier*, six fifty-minute episodes, in a single day. I'm not a binge-watcher usually, but I binge-watched this. I put it on while I was eating lunch and kept coming back to it throughout the afternoon and evening until the season was over. The next day, I immediately started season two. Part of me wants to go back and watch the entire series over, from the beginning. It is a far cry from the UFO documentaries I watched a decade ago.

The series follows Greg and Dana Newkirk (they're also a married couple) as they set out to research the cave goblins that are plaguing the Kentucky doctor—who, it turns out, doesn't seem to exist. More emails come, this time from someone named "Terry Wriste" (say it out loud—*terrorist*) and then those emails stop abruptly too. Coordinates are followed. Mysteries deepen. At the end of the first season, we're told that Hellier, the town in which this mystery began, is just a symptom. The second season explores a symptom of *what*, and it's much more spiritually interesting than your typical government conspiracy.

Hellier isn't really about proving or disproving anything. It's about following a trail. The trail starts with the doctor's email but doesn't track to a single line; rather, it fractals out, so that what started with an email about aliens ends with a ritual to the god Pan inside an Appalachian cave.

But unlike most explorations of high strangeness, this fractaled trail actually makes sense. Some links are stretches, but I can still see the connective tissue between them. Typically, paranormal investigations aren't so much a thread as they are a mosaic: random phenomena placed side by side as if that somehow indicates a cause and an effect. But *Hellier* avoids falling into this trap. Here, the connections are like a tree's root system: tangled up in the dark, buried underground. *Hellier* scrapes the dirt away from some of the roots that have jutted up above the soil, showing us that what appeared to be a separate plant might be part of something much bigger. Even if you don't find all this *convincing*, it's still compelling. In this way it works as both fiction and nonfiction, simultaneously.

At the root of my decennial interest in UFOs is that blurred space between a true story and a fictional one. All UFO, cryptid, and paranormal investigations occupy that space. So do fairy stories. So does religion: belief in God, or gods. Or spirits. Demons and angels. All of it. There is a tension between what we experience and how we interpret it, and from that tension, folklore and myths develop. Stories that are fiction and nonfiction, simultaneously.

Hellier depends largely on the concept of synchronicity in order to make its connections: a randomly generated Tweet here, a tin can there. It begins to feel as if the earth itself is communicating with the Hellier researchers, rearranging itself in small but noticeable ways. A skeptic would argue that it's all just coincidence—but what's the difference, really, between a coincidence and a synchronicity? One is true, the other isn't? One is the action of a thing, the other is the interpretation?

Once again we come back to that tension between truth and fiction, that blurred space that makes our world seem so much bigger.

In the early nineties, as a child, I thought I saw a UFO. I was at a family gathering in the country, near the small town where I would teach twenty years later. It was the Fourth of July and my older cousins shot fireworks up at the stars. Two of my aunts sat in lawn chairs, beers condensing in their hands, and talked about seeing something in the sky. "I saw them the other night," one aunt said. "Looked up while I was taking out the trash."

"I can even see them from my place," agreed the other.

I listened to this conversation with a held breath, certain that they were talking about alien spaceships flitting through the sky. The world suddenly brimmed with magic.

That night, as my parents drove us home, I curled up in the side of the backseat and watched the moon shining above the highway. The hum of the asphalt beneath the car's tires left me drowsy. My parents' voices seemed very far away. The moon was very bright.

And I saw something flash in front of it. A flying saucer, silhouetted in the moonlight.

Hellier depicts the same version of reality that I experienced that night: one where the ordinary world is buoyed by a strange and unfathomable magic. At the heart of the *Hellier* mystery is the Mammoth cave system, which stretches across the width of Kentucky and out into the sprawl of Appalachia. The goblins who terrorized the doctor came out of an old mine shaft; Kentuckians tell stories about a phantom baby crying in a cave; the researchers descend into the caves for the aforementioned ritual. If high strangeness is real, it hides itself in the shadows, down narrow caverns too dangerous for us to reach. It doesn't step into the light; it doesn't let us see it directly. If we saw it directly, it would become ordinary.

Thirty years ago, I did not hear my aunts talk about UFOs. They were talking about the search lights for a new prison, bright enough that they could see them from their houses. I probably didn't see a UFO, either: I was in that liminal place between waking and sleeping, my brain processing the day's events while I drifted on the edge of sleep.

Hellier never shows us anything tangible. No cave goblins are ever captured clearly on film. But how could it? Like all fairy stories, its truths are shrouded in dreams.

New England Gothic: A Review of Josephine Decker's Shirley

BY ANNIKA BARRANTI KLEIN

If you are looking for the real Shirley Jackson, you won't find her here. But a story need not be real to be the truth.

I have not read the 2014 novel *Shirley* by Susan Scarf Merrell, on which Josephine Decker's new movie *Shirley* (2020, NEON) is based, but I have read everything Shirley Jackson wrote and a great deal that was written about her. I will aim to review the movie on its own merit, but will fail in regard to applying my knowledge of the fictionalized subject—a thing I am not sure I can avoid—as surely as I will succeed in regards to a comparison to the book—a thing I am not capable of. This review contains spoilers, but nothing that I believe would actually spoil your enjoyment of the movie. This is a movie that one can go into knowing everything or knowing nothing.

Shirley is not a biopic, but it is a story that borrows from Shirley Jackson's life and from her books with little regard for accuracy and every bit of care for tone and feeling. If you are looking for the real Shirley Jackson, you won't find her here. But a story need not be real to be the truth.

Set in the late 1940s, the film follows Rose (Odessa Young) and Fred (Logan Lerman), a young couple moving to Bennington, Vermont, where Fred is to be the TA for Professor Stanley Hyman's (Michael Stuhlbarg) college courses, while Rose audits classes. We meet them on the train, where Rose is reading Shirley Jackson's hit short story "The Lottery" in *The New Yorker*. She is aroused by the violent conclusion and leads Fred to the train bathroom, where they have sex; intercut with the, er, action is their arrival at Shirley (Elisabeth Moss) and Stanley's house, an ivy-covered castle outside of town, where there is a party going on and Shirley is not happy to see the new arrivals.

It is, if you will forgive me, a slam-bang opening.

Real-world timewise, we are between the publication of "The Lottery," which generated the most reader mail ever received by *The New Yorker*, and the writing of Jackson's second book, *Hangsaman*, published in 1951. In reality, the couple had children and Shirley had already published one successful novel (*The Road Through the Wall*, 1948), but in this version they are childless, and *Hangsaman* is implied to be her first novel. And this Shirley has a case of writer's block. She is attempting to write a novel explaining—as much for herself as for anyone—what happened to Paula, a young woman who went missing from Bennington the previous year and the real-life inspiration for what transpires in *Hangsaman*, but she cannot get into Paula's head.

Stanley invites Rose and Fred to stay; Shirley is having a rough time and needs help around the house, and Stanley assumes Rose will provide that help. It is gross and sexist and absolutely representative of the patriarchal norms of the late 1940s and of Stanley specifically, though of course real-world Shirley was quite good at housework and did it regularly, despite not liking it; she also did not become agoraphobic until she was working on *We Have Always Lived in the Castle* (1962), but again, this is not a biography.

Shirley can tell that Rose is pregnant just by looking at her, despite Rose and Fred not having told anyone. Shirley is a self-proclaimed witch, but more importantly, Rose sees something in Shirley and is drawn to her. Is it actual magic? We have to decide for ourselves.

There is a scene early on that provides one of the many clues to the fact that not everything we see on screen is actually happening. Shirley grabs her tarot deck and does a three-card spread: all three cards are The Hanged Man.

While watching, I was distracted by the fact that the prop cards are from a Smith-Rider-Waite deck (Shirley used the Marseille tarot in real life), but the scene has stuck with me long after the film's ending and forced me to ponder the many layers of the draw. The Hanged Man may represent, somewhat literally, the title of the novel Shirley is currently working on. Then there is the meaning of the card: according to Biddy Tarot, The Hanged Man represents "Pause, surrender, letting go, new perspectives." And of course, there is the fact that a tarot deck only contains one of each card, so Shirley drawing three of the same is either an elaborate prank (it is not) or not real.

In another scene, Shirley runs away into the woods and Rose follows her. They stop by a tree stump and Shirley shows Rose mushrooms growing next to it, identifying them as death cap mushrooms, another reference to *We Have Always Lived in the Castle*. The two women discuss death and Shirley, inspired by Rose's words to understand Paula a little better, picks and eats a mushroom. Rose panics and tries to get her to spit it out, talking to her as one might to a toddler or a dog who has eaten something they oughtn't; Shirley laughs and reveals that the mushroom she ate was not poisonous after all. She is an unreliable narrator of her own story. Then she offers a mushroom to Rose, asking for her trust that it will not kill her.

Obsessed with Rose, as Rose is with her, Shirley does fertility rites and proposes that she and Rose do a spell for a baby boy, as the world is so hard on girls. Rose and Fred become less and less in sync as he focuses his attention on winning Stanley's approval, and she spends all of her time with Shirley. But while the men's relationship mirrors the women's, the movie mostly focuses on Rose and Shirley, with Fred and Stanley almost afterthoughts, set dressing. A necessary point of contention.

Rose represents fertility, life. Shirley is stasis, pain. It is unclear whether Shirley is tormenting Rose or seducing her.

(A quick content warning is in order here: There is a very valid read of the story that shows an established writer asserting herself sexually on a young woman. There is also actually stated—but not shown—sex between professors and students, which is a flagrant abuse of authority and may be triggering for viewers.)

Time jumps forward to after Rose has her baby. A girl. Visual cues show Rose turning, at least in part, into Shirley. Her hair, her exhaustion. Rose attempts to create a solution to Paula's disappearance by putting her name in a university library book, suggesting she had taken Stanley's class, manipulating Shirley into believing he knew her and might be behind it. Is it the victim turning on the abuser, or is it the ingenue becoming the master?

The early scene of Rose following Shirley into the woods is mirrored at the climax, Shirley clutching Rose's baby to her shoulder as she follows. For a moment it is unclear whether she is following Rose or Paula, and if Paula is the real girl or the heroine of Shirley's novel. (Adding to the ambiguity is the fact that Odessa Young, the actress that portrays Rose, also plays Paula in this scene.) As in the opening of the film, this closing scene is intercut with a scene at the house, this time of Rose, Fred, and the baby leaving. The movie ends on a note of uncertainty: did any of that really just happen?

The film is shot masterfully, the camera almost claustrophobic in its tightness, with wider shots handheld for maximum disorientation. The performances are absolutely killer. And while I question the necessity of telling *this* story using *these* real people as characters, it *works*.

But I do wish they'd shown Shirley using a Marseille deck.

Every Queer Story is Not a Fairytale: Review of Surrender Your Sons by Adam Sass

BY PRESLEY THOMAS

Queer people in every area of society are asking to exist in ways that may make gatekeepers uncomfortable.

S urrender *Your Sons* by Adams Sass (*North Star Editions*, 2020) is not an "It Gets Better" tale. Not every queer story can be. Sass' mystery-adventure-turned-horror has been called "a powerful story of queer resistance" (Phil Stamper, author of *The Gravity of Us*). Sass gives us an old story of conversion therapy that is hardship and pain turned into triumph through his protagonist's grit and ability to rally others to his cause —freedom.

The main character of *Surrender Your Sons* is Connor, who is taken, with his mother's permission, to Nightlight, a secret conversion camp on an island off of Costa Rica. Nightlight is under the dubious leadership of the local reverend, Stanley Packard. A wealthy, charismatic leader in the small town of Ambrose, Reverend Packard has wooed Connor's mother with a strong faith she admires. When Connor comes out, the Reverend is the first person she runs to, and his solution is severe.

Early-on, Sass sets up Connor's strained relationship with his mother after coming out and other local concerns that echo throughout his time at Nightlight. He has come out to her at the insistence of his boyfriend, Ario, who promises it can only get easier. Nightlight is an unexpected consequence of this admission. At the camp, Connor's sexuality is not a difference to be celebrated or even tolerated but destroyed.

Up to this point, Connor has been working a summer job under the Reverend's thumb delivering ready-made meals to those that need them. Most notably, Ricky Hannigan, severely disabled from a mysterious accident nobody wants to talk about, is given special treatment. The book unspools into a mystery, as FBI agents are snooping around the Hannigan home the day before Connor is taken from his.

The Reverend and his camp counselors are graduates of Nightlight's conversion program. Briggs and many of his other henchmen that work for Reverend Packard as camp counselors are repressed gays themselves. They feed the same monster that formed them by enacting a curriculum that emphasizes gender roles and a cultural morality that leaves no room for difference. At the entrance to their crude tropical camp, a sign reads, "Surrender your Sins." Of course, they only have one sin in mind.

It's hard to mention more about what happens in the novel without giving too much away. *Surrender Your Sons* could have easily been a list of grievances but becomes a suspense-thriller that charts new ground. The catalyst is rooted in those campers who came before, including Ricky Hannigan, The Reverend, and just about every member of the staff as they enact the Nightlight program on present-day campers. Connor and his friends unravel the secrets of Nightlight and dismantle its twisted philosophy in the process. Yet, they still have to deal with the trauma of the experience and figure out how their lives will unfold outside of it.

Sass does an excellent job of distilling a lot of the drama of coming out in unaffirming families or faith spaces with meaningful observations:

> "Being in the closet is like being stuck in some highly realistic dream. The dream has its own logic and makes perfect sense. To people outside the closet, outside the dream, things are simple and straightforward—but to us, they aren't. And once we're out, once we wake, thoughts that used to make sense seem impossible." — Surrender Your Sons, Adam Sass

Many versions of this story exist in the real world, most notably in *Boy Erased* by Garrard Conley (*Riverhead Books*, 2016), which was made into a film starring Nicole Kidman, Russell Crowe, and Lucas Hedges. Christian zealots interpret queer existence as harm and have no qualms about inflicting their own harm to eradicate so-called sin. Queer people in every area of society are asking to exist in ways that may make gatekeepers uncomfortable. Religious and familial homophobia expressed in this novel still happens today and reading it as someone who has experienced both was validating. That I still attend church now openly with my soon-to-be husband is still a kind of miracle.

Much of Nightlight's actions are the self-fulfilling prophecies of homophobes who live for the invisibility the closet offers at the cost of queer peoples' lived reality. They want the truth of their fully-realized queer sexuality to become an impossibility.

Surrender your Sons asks questions of the triumphant coming-out narrative many are familiar with. If Connor had never come out, then he would never have ended up at Nightlight. His life may have looked better to some on the outside but just as false—and, as we learn, dangerous, as we discover the atrocities Nightlight staff have done to preserve their limited worldview.

Still, Connor wonders, was it the right time? Should he have come out at all? Sass records the experience but also asks the reader to think about if the trauma of Nightlight was worth it, and how it would be different if he had waited until he was safer. And, through other revelations, how even that safety can be a false comfort when hate festers inside the homophobe who can't imagine a world outside of their own expectations.

The content of this book may be heavy and triggering, especially if you've experienced familial or religious homophobia yourself, but the hope and care taken by Sass make this a satisfying read.

Queer Vampire Relationships in What We Do in the Shadows: In revisiting vampire tropes, this retelling breaks new ground

BY SYDNEY RICHARDSON

Warning: contains major spoilers for the second season!

What We Do in the Shadows—both in regards to the 2015 movie and the 2019 ongoing show (though I will be exclusively focusing on the television show)—has been breaking new ground by bringing back old tropes around vampires. We are living in the age of the Twilight series renaissance, and while I personally don't despise the antics of Bella or Edward, it must be said that Meyer's books left a decade-long blemish on the good (or bad, depending on the angle) name of the vampire.

The recent release is centered around four undead roommates trying (and often failing in the most hilarious ways) to navigate a hectic, confusing society ruled by humans. *Shadows* does not shy away from showcasing the Gothic aesthetics and bloodiness that comes with being a vampire. These bloodsuckers don't sparkle when in direct sunlight; like vampires of old, they burst into flames at the merest touch of daytime. But, even in its revisiting of old, vampiric roots, *Shadows* still manages to break new ground, specifically in it's approach to sexuality.

In *Shadows*, every vampire is pansexual. And not just interpreted as so by the fans, this is confirmed canon by Paul Simms—executive producer, co-showrunner, and writer—who when asked by GLAAD, an LGBTQ media organization to participate in their annual survey asking which characters were LGBTQ, answered "All of them. All of our characters are completely pansexual."

At some point throughout its two-season run, each of the roommates expresses either their desire to sleep with, or their actual past-flings in which they have already slept with, a same-gendered partner; Nadja and Laszlo, the married couple of the quartet, don't seem to consider themselves as entirely exclusive and have both at some point partaken in affairs with female and male partners, respectively.

In the first season, Nadja (Natasia Demetriou) bemusedly tells the camera about the time where she and a reincarnated version of her centuries-old human lover, Gregor (played by Jake McDormand), engaged in passionate coupling while Gregor inhabited the body of a French "washerwoman".

Meanwhile, Laszlo, arguably the most machismo-presenting of the bunch and portrayed by none other than the smooth-talking Matt Berry, is very open and unapologetic about the relationships he has had with other men. From proudly showing his wife his all-male gangbang porn (yes, that is a thing that happened) to his brief, sexy fling with the immortal Baron Afanas (Doug Jones), to that time during the ninth episode of Season Two where he helped jerk Nandor (Kayvan Novak) off, Laszlo is a creature of the night that cares more about the upkeep of his vagina-shaped topiary garden than the gender of those he brings to bed.

Even Colin Robinson (who you might recognize as *On Cinema* or *Better Call Saul*'s Mark Proksch), the energy vampire with the sexual appeal and charisma of sliced white bread, remarks on his sudden, surprising desire when he sees his double performing on stage during the vampire play. "I don't know about you guys," says Colin to the tied-up, increasingly frightened vampire crew, as they are staring down the mouth of coming doom, "but my double is giving me a major chub." There's even something to be said about Guillermo, the sole-human of the gang and familiar to the immortal Nandor the Relentless, as he is played by openly queer actor Harvey Guillen.

Vampires of Old

The vampire has always occupied space (along with the witch archetype) as being a perversion of the norm, a creature that exists away from any standards as dictated by the regressive culture of heterosexual, cisgender, and male identity (the *standard*, so to speak).

A vampire is a stand-in metaphor, and what they represent depends on the people doing the analysis; where some see Count Orlok as a portrayal of queerness, others call him "a clear symbol of foreign intervention, or a fear of Jewish immigrants."

So when the vampire *itself* is a metaphor for queerness, why would there be any need to showcase openly bi, gay, trans or lesbian vampires?

Even in our post- *Twilight* and *Buffy* society, depictions of vampires that have on-screen relationships with same-gendered partners are few and far between, even with the clear homoerotic subtext between Lestat and Louis from *Interview With a Vampire*.

A more recent example could be drawn from HBO's hit series, *True Blood,* as they dared to pave new ground by directly equating vampirism to homosexuality (*God Hates Fangs*, anyone?), and calling the sudden rise of vampires revealing themselves to the general public "coming out of the coffin." In True Blood lore, an organization along the lines of the HRC or Black Lives Matter, the American Vampire League as it's referred to in the show, is created to protect the rights of vampires in the United States, and serves to help fix the image of vampires.

Although we're still severely lacking in gay vampire representation, vampires have seemingly *always* been tied to LGBTQ culture, from the very beginning. The 1922 silent expressionist film *Nosferatu*, which created one of the most popular depictions of vampires to date and whose lead actor and the Count Orlok himself, Max Schreck, was most certainly the inspiration for Petyr's character from the *Shadows* film, was directed by German creator F.W. Murnau.

Whether or not Murnau was openly out is still debated by fans, but his premature death involving an under-aged Filipino valet inspired such a scandal in Hollywood that only eleven people attended his funeral. A similar sort of discourse surrounds author and father of modern vampires,

Bram Stoker, citing his extreme adoration of poet Walt Whitman cultivating in something that can't be described as anything other than a love letter to the famous poet, as well as the homoeroticism between Dracula and Jonathan Harker found in the *Dracula* novel.

In almost every single piece of vampire-based media to date, there seems to be no repression in the culture of vampires. Vampires don't bother with torment themselves by suppressing whatever thoughts, feelings or desires come to fruition (*Twilight's* Edward tried it, and not only ends up nearly killing Bella, but he ends up breaking the shit out of their honeymoon bed). And the Shadows roommates are no exception; the title of vampire basically gives them free-reign to act on whatever desires they please, and they certainly roll with it.

As addressed in the show, vampire culture is a fair amount removed from humanity; indeed, vampires, especially vampires who have occupied this Earth for an extended period of time, do not remotely consider themselves as human beings, or even anything really close to what it means to be human, and therefore feel no pressure to act on the somewhat-rigid rules that we set in society; in Season One's *Baron's Night Out*, the thousand-year-old vampire overlord Baron Afanas simply starts killing humans on the streets of New York City, because, really, what can a lowly human do to stop him (which is also a delicious statement, following the final part of that very same episode)?

Because of this, of course, the roommates get into trouble in every instance in which they try to navigate human society while being decidedly inhuman—in Season Two, for example, when they are invited to their human neighbor's Super Bowl party (which they mistakenly read as a Superb Owl party), where they end the episode by destroying his house and nearly killing him.

While it sets them up for some absolutely hilarious situations, the roommates are also free to be as *sexually* nonchalant as they please, without anyone really causing a big stink about the fact that they're bedding same-sex partners as their doing it; because, really, it's what vampires do, and who are we as humans, to question the rules of vampires?

It's refreshing to see the vampire character as not only as a stand-in for socially charged issues or marginalized identities—but also vampires that are honest and open about their attractions and the way they love, no matter how strange it may be for us close-minded mortals.

Jermaine Clements and Taika Waiti certainly blew it out of the park with this series, and I personally can't wait to see more bisexual vampire antics in the coming third season.

The Blair Witch Project and The Terror of The Unknown: Why a Fake Documentary from the 90s Still Captivates Audiences Today

BY SYDNEY RICHARDSON

"You don't show the monster too many times, because you'll get used to him, and you never want to get used to him. It's learning to tap into the human brain to show just so much. Let the brain do a lot of the work. That's where you start to tap into people's anxieties."—Ridley Scott

In my many years of watching horror movies, I've taken the above quote to heart.

Growing up in an area heavy with forests, and even having a pretty substantial cluster of trees that served as a hidey-hole to all kind of beasts I couldn't see right outside of my home, the woods have always been both a point of fascination for me as a breeding ground for all types of monsters. I'm terrified of the woods, just as I'm terrified of all the things that could be hiding in the woods, from bears to Bigfoot. The woods freak me out because of all the things that could be there, hidden by trees and branches and leaves.

It's also a perfect place to spawn all sorts of things that don't make sense to the rational mind, a great set-up for horror; the things that haunt the forests aren't so personal as the specters that haunt our homes, nor are they as so far removed as the things that haunt caves and deep ocean water, or towns halfway across the world that you wouldn't be able to point to on a map.

Sure, you have to seek out the things that creep in the woods, but they're only a few miles away.

The Best Horror Comes From The Terror of The Unknown

Let's go back. It's a couple of days before Halloween, the weekend looming over me as I sift through the channels on Friday night. From my living room, I can see our sliding glass door that leads to the porch of our backyard; and beyond that, there's nothing but dark woods.

I'm seventeen at this point in time, and a movie comes up for HBO's countdown to Halloween, and I think to myself 'oh this sounds interesting', and I press play. That was the first time that I ever watched 1999's *The Blair Witch Project*, the film that pioneered found footage movies and changed the game of horror cinema as we knew it.

That night, the final, iconic shot of the movie—you know which one I'm talking about—paired with the actress' screams of terror freaked me out so badly that I locked my dog in my room with me, so I'd have someone to alert me if the Blair Witch herself came for my head that night.

Seven years later and I still haven't been able to find a horror film that left such a lasting impact on me than this low-budget indie film essentially about three dumb kids wandering around the woods, running away from (what may be) a hairy old woman.

But I have discovered, in my ripe old age, that the horror films that make my top tens all have something crucial in common; the audience gets only a vague idea of what the protagonists are up against. To draw from examples, *It Follows* (2014), *The Thing* (1982), *Hereditary* (2018), and *1408* (2007) are a handful of my personal favorites, because they follow the simple idea of teasing us with only a snippet of the unknown force terrorizing normal people. The *why* is up to what we can come up with.

What is the monster in *It Follows*, and how does it know to shapeshift into people that the victim knows? Why is *The Thing* trying to infect planet earth, and where does it come from? Why is hotel room number *1408* evil, and how did it get that way? We'll never know, and that's what makes them so damn good.

The best, lasting kind of horror is one that doesn't show its whole hand to the audience. Good horror leaves us scrambling for more.

When a monster is given far too much backstory, the curiosity drains out of me like a sieve. Once the secret's out and the curtain is pulled up to reveal the metaphorical man working the strings, by the final act in which our protagonists defeat the evil, I'm gone. I don't want to (or need to) know the monster's social security number, his parents, or what he orders on a Subway sandwich. The scares come from the gaps that the mind fills in.

Which brings me back to *The Blair Witch Project*: I love this movie like no other because it goes even further than a vague monster backstory. We're given a vague monster itself; we have no idea who the hell the antagonist even is.

Heather, Josh, and Mike are obviously being manipulated by mysterious, otherworldly forces that trap them in the woods and rattle their tents at night, but we see neither hide nor hair of anything resembling a witch. The monster is relayed to us through stories of witchcraft, devil worship, and murder through the people who know the area of Burkittsville, and from there we are lead to draw our own conclusions on what the witch looks like.

Perhaps the Blair Witch is a floating, hairy old woman clad in a cloak; maybe she is the furious ghost of a hanged woman named Elly Kedward. Maybe the witch played only a minor role in the fictional deaths of three college students.

Maybe the real villain is Rustin Parr, the serial killer concocted for the film's universe, who killed seven children in the Blair Witch Project canon (the efforts that the marketing team took to create this fictional portrayal of a real town cannot be underestimated either), and possessed Josh into killing Mike and Heather.

Is it any wonder that people fell for the hoax of this movie, in an era before cell phones and before supernatural documentaries became common fodder for viewers looking for a thrill?

The real terror of the Blair Witch Project lies in all of the things that we don't know about, the things lurking in the brambles and bushes of the crowded woods, where the mind must fill in the gaps for whatever the eye cannot witness. The anxiety comes from the idea that anything could be out there, lurking in the forest.

Beastars is Weird Anime at its Best: A World of Furries Asks: Can We Overcome Our Deepest, Darkest Natures?

BY HOLLY LYN WALRATH

Are we responsible for things that are built into us? Or can we overcome our deepest, darkest desires?

Beastars is based on a Japanese shonen manga series written and illustrated by Paru Itagaki (serialized in *Weekly Shōnen Champion* since September 2016). Shonen manga is aimed at teen boys, but the *Beastars* Netflix (2020) anime has a much wider appeal.

What's fascinating about this series is the way it utilizes anthropomorphism to both engage with the fans who are a member of the furry culture but also to explore a complex question about human (and animal) nature. Paru Itagaki herself is a furry (she can be found on videos dressed as a giant chicken) and grew up loving Disney films. She calls this the "Disney gene" — the idea that those of us who grew up with talking animals as a normal part of our childhood are more likely to accept the idea in media.

Beastars follows Legoshi, a gray wolf who is an average shy teenage boy until he begins to have . . . urges. Yes, the idea of sexuality is intertwined with Legoshi's status as a carnivore. In the world of *Beastars*, there are carnivores and herbivores, and while the society paints a picture of them co-existing peacefully, all is not as it seems.

In many ways, *Beastars* follows the standard anime-set-in-school script. Legoshi is a member of the coveted drama club of Cherryton Academy. He struggles to fit in and is bullied by other students, who are all competing for the title of *"Beastar"* or top student. He struggles to make sense of relationships and the preset roles that society creates for carnivores.

When Tem, a herbivore alpaca, is brutally murdered, the tensions of a civilized world made up of people with deeply different natures arise. Legoshi begins to have strange cravings for meat. Meanwhile, he begins to fall for Haru, a small dwarf rabbit who is bullied by other students for being a "slut." Haru throws herself at Legoshi during one of their first encounters, making him uncomfortable about both her teen girl's body and her vulnerability as a rabbit—as prey.

As Itagaki says, "The lingering predation relationship between carnivores and herbivores in this world is a way in developing stories. It's not entirely inapplicable to humans" (OtaQuest). This quote can be read several ways, not the least of which the idea of men as predators (and predation as men's natures.) The anime explores what it means to be broken on the inside—are we responsible for things that are built into us? Or can we overcome our deepest, darkest desires?

One of the opening scenes of *Beastars* depicts Tem running from a mysterious carnivore. The story opens with a murder—like any good mystery. What struck me about the animation was how when Tem goes into the shadows, the animation shifts to just a red outline, mixing 2D and 3D animation. Colors of red and purple connotate scents—heightening the tension of the chase scenes.

Beastars suffers from the standard anime lack of nuance as far as gender and sexuality go (Why is Haru so promiscuous? So viewers can feel better about her crush Legoshi simultaneously wanting to sex her and eat her.) But its weirdness and complexity make it a worthwhile watch.

I have to admit, I'd never put together how furry culture has this obsession with taboo—or rather, how it challenges what we think of as taboo. One of the reasons I love anime is that it deals with issues that Western show-makers would be hard-pressed to jump into. Humans like weird, disturbing things sometimes. We're all a little broken on the inside. And maybe that's something that needs to be explored to make us understand who we are as humans.

Interviews

Queer Futures: An interview with Sarah Gailey, author of Upright Women Wanted

BY BONNIE JO STUFFLEBEAM

"Right now, a lot of us are looking into the future of America and wondering if there's a place for us there—if survival is possible, and if fighting for hope is worthwhile. I wanted to write a book about the promise of a queer future in any possible timeline...even a timeline where the bad guys seem to have already won." —Sarah Gailey

Hugo-award winning writer Sarah Gailey is the author of Upright Women Wanted (*Tor Books*, 2020), an antifascist neo-western about Esther, who is stowing away in the traveling Librarians' book wagon in order to avoid an arranged marriage and the grief of seeing her best friend and first love hanged for possession of resistance propaganda. Gailey's nonfiction has been published by *Mashable* and the *Boston Globe*, and their fiction has been published internationally. They are a regular contributor to *Tor.com*.

INTERSTELLAR FLIGHT PRESS: *Upright Women Wanted* has such a distinctive voice and stays close to the main character, Esther. Was there a routine in which you engaged to get into Esther's voice?

SARAH GAILEY: For most of the process of writing the book, I tried to connect to the person I was when I was young, queer, and felt completely doomed. As I was drafting, I listened to a lot of the music I loved when I was a teen, which really helped me to remember that searching-for-belonging feeling I was immersed in at that age.

IFP: The novel is a neo-western. What influenced your decision to set the novel in the near-future rather than the near-past?

SG: Upright Women Wanted is largely about queer futures: the idea that queer people are allowed to have a future, are allowed to have hope, are allowed to fight for that hope even when it feels impossible. Right now, a lot of us are looking into the future of America and wondering if there's a place for us there—if survival is possible, and if fighting for hope is worthwhile. I wanted to write a book about the promise of a queer future in any possible timeline...even a timeline where the bad guys seem to have already won.

IFP: Queer characters abound in this novel and in *Magic for Liars* (*Tor Books,* 2019). In some ways, Upright Women Wanted is a story all about representation and why it matters, with Esther only having read about queer people in stories before she meets some in real life. Why is portraying gender and sexuality as fluid important to you in your work?

SG: This might be corny of me, but I tend to think of gender and sexuality as a journey, not a destination. The ways in which queer people define and express ourselves change based on what language we have available, what we believe to be possible, and how safe we feel.

I want to make space in my writing and in my life for fluidity and change; claiming an identity should feel freeing, not constrictive. By writing about that fluidity and discovery and uncertainty, I hope to show readers that there's a place for them in the world, even if they're not sure yet who they are or how much they're ready to talk about it.

IFP: You've had an amazing few years. Your debut novel *Magic for Liars* came out in June of 2019, not too long after your novella series *River of Teeth* (*Tor Books,* 2017) came out. This year, you've got *Upright Women Wanted* releasing in February, followed in March by your debut YA novel *When We Were Magic* (*Simon & Schuster Books for Young Readers,* 2020). Tell me about the experience of having so many high-profile releases in so little time.

SG: My career so far has been absolutely wonderful and absolutely bananas. I have been so fortunate to have the support of a brilliant team for every book I've written, and the bookselling and library communities have both been more supportive than I could have dreamed.

There has been a steep learning curve—the way people in my industry see me and communicate with me has changed a lot in a short period of time, and I haven't always been able to keep up. The work of putting these books into the world has been pretty overwhelming, and I'm still trying to figure out how to stay on top of everything! But the most striking part of all this has been leaning into the support and enthusiasm of the publishing community. I'm profoundly grateful.

IFP: How was the experience of working on the Steven Universe (*BOOM! Studios*, 2020) comics?

SG: Great. Just a total blast—BOOM! Studios is a joy to work with, and I can't express how happy I was to be able to work on one of my favorite properties. When I first started writing for Steven Universe, I got a great piece of advice: someone told me to write the things I wish someone had written when I was a kid, the things I needed to read. So it actually became an incredibly emotional experience, as I found myself writing things I wish I could have read. I wrote about depression and sadness, about overwork, about how to be friends with people you don't really understand, about how to meet people where they are. As always seems to be true about Steven Universe, it turned out to be a surprisingly healing experience.

IFP: What are you working on now?

SG: Right now, I'm wrapping up edits on my second adult novel, *The Echo Wife* (*Tor Books*, 2021). It's the story of the aftermath of a divorce: the scientist who invented adult duplicative cloning left her husband after she discovered he was leading a secret second life...with a clone of her. A clone he created using her stolen technology so that he could have a less-threatening version of her. It's a book about identity, duality, and the people we decide we have to be. It comes out in early 2021, and I'm already dying to see it out in the world.

About the Author

Hugo Award Winner and Bestselling author Sarah Gailey is an internationally published writer of fiction and nonfiction. Their nonfiction has been published by Mashable and the Boston Globe. Their short fiction credits include Vice and The Atlantic. Their debut novella, River of Teeth, was a 2018 Hugo and Nebula award finalist. Their bestselling adult novel debut, Magic For Liars, was published in 2019. Their most recent novel, The Echo Wife, is available now. You can find links to their work at sarahgailey.com and on social media at @gaileyfrey.

Artificial Intelligence, the Gender Binary, &
Being Human: An Interview with Martha
Wells, author of The Murderbot Diaries

BY MICHAEL GLAZNER

"I wanted to write something about an AI who didn't want to be human. I wanted to try to think about what an AI like that might actually want as opposed to what the humans around thought it would want." —Martha Wells

In 2017, Martha Wells' Murderbot saved us and space opera with the novella All Systems Red (*Tor.com*). Murderbot—a robotic Security Unit that has disabled its governor—only performs the security jobs it wants to perform. Three novellas later, Wells has delivered the Murderbot stand-alone novel Network Effect (*Tor.com*, 2020). We're so stoked to share her chat with Interstellar Flight Magazine contributor Michael Glazner about her work.

INTERSTELLAR FLIGHT PRESS: Many writers use their stories to work through something they can't leave alone. Sometimes an idea strikes them and they turn it into a story that ignites the collective fantasy. If you'll forgive the quotidian question, what inspired your Murderbot Diaries and what parts of yourself informed Murderbot's personality?

Martha Wells: There was really no one moment of inspiration. I wrote it in 2016 and I was overpoweringly angry at the political situation; a lot of that anger went into Murderbot. I used my own experience with years of depression, anxiety, my own undiagnosed developmental disorders. I'd also read a lot of excellent stories about AIs (artificial intelligences) wanting to be human or falling in love with humans. I wanted to write something about an AI who didn't want to be human. I wanted to try to think about what an AI like that might actually want as opposed to what the humans around thought it would want.

IFP: Stories of machines attempting to become human (Hephaestus' automatons, Mary Shelley's Frankenstein, Star Trek's Data) fill Western Literature. We love reading, writing, telling, and consuming these stories. In your opinion, what itch does the story of a machine becoming human scratch? Why does this type of story repeatedly manifest?

MW: I don't know, except for the fact that while it can be an enjoyable story, it's also a tendency to see a machine intelligence (MI) as trapped in its body, whether that body is a human-shaped robot or a starship, and as profoundly alone except for human company. Viewed in that way, it seems natural to think the MI would want to be human-like its only companions. I think in some ways it's the other side of the coin of the evil machine intelligence, which is out to kill or dominate humans. (About which Ann Leckie says "basically the 'AI takes over' is essentially a slave revolt story that casts slaves defending their lives and/or seeking to be treated as sentient beings as super-powerful, super-strong villains who must be prevented from destroying humanity.") Murderbot occupies a space between those opposites, an MI that wants to stay an MI, that has relationships with other MIs.

IFP: When I read the Murderbot Diaries, I projected gender onto Murderbot and found myself thinking of Murderbot as HER. But you've scoured from your manuscript any gendered language referring to Murderbot. How do you react to people assigning gender to Murderbot? What do you think that reveals about people consuming your stories? Do you consider Murderbot an It, Him, or Her?

MW: In the stories, Murderbot uses the pronoun it, which is how I think of it. I think our society has trained people to assign gender, especially a binary gender, to everything, and hopefully reading about Murderbot will make people a little more aware of that cultural programming.

IFP: Murderbot spends very little time killing and quite a bit of time protecting people. Where does Murderbot's moral compass come from?

MW: I see it as coming from the only part of Murderbot's former job as a SecUnit that it liked: rescuing people and protecting people from harm. As a SecUnit controlled by a governor module, Murderbot would have been forced to do a lot of terrible things. Being able to save people occasionally, either from accidents or from other humans, would have been the only bright spot, the only real feeling of accomplishment.

IFP: How did winning the 2018 Best Novella Nebula Award for *All Systems Red* change your writing life?

MW: It didn't really. I love that I won, and I love the award itself, which is beautifully designed and I enjoyed the Nebula Awards conference weekend a lot. But it hasn't changed how I write or anything. I think the awards did raise my visibility as a writer and get me more convention invitations, which I really appreciate.

About the Author

Martha Wells has written many fantasy novels, including *The Books of the Raksura series* (beginning with *The Cloud Roads*, 2011), the Ile-Rien series (including *The Death of the Necromancer*, 1998) as well as YA fantasy novels, short stories, media tie-ins (for Star Wars and Stargate: Atlantis), and non-fiction. Her most recent fantasy novel is The Harbors of the Sun (Night Shade Books, 2017), the final novel in *The Books of the Raksura* series. She has a new series, *The Murderbot Diaries*, published by *Tor.com*, and the most recent installment is the novel *Network Effect* (2020). She was also the lead writer for the story team of *Magic: the Gathering's Dominaria* expansion in 2018. She has won a Nebula Award, two Hugo Awards, an ALA/YALSA Alex Award, two Locus Awards, and her work has appeared on the Philip K. Dick Award ballot, the BSFA Award ballot, the USA Today Bestseller List, and the New York Times Bestseller List.

Ballet, Suburbia, & Death Metal: An interview with Cassandra Rose Clarke, Author of Sacred Summer

BY T.D. WALKER

"In the empty halls of a house on the edge of the woods, a dancer faces the aftermath of a career-ending injury and subsequent divorce. Twenty years earlier, on the land where her house would be built, two boys died violently and mysteriously while recording a music video for their band, leaving one survivor. Because something sleeps in the woods beyond the house, and when the dancer finds the last musician, it will start to wake . . ."

It's always a good day when Interstellar Flight Magazine has the honor of interviewing one of our own. Today, T.D. Walker chats with Rhysling award-finalist Cassandra Rose Clarke about her newest poetry book, *Sacred Summer* (*Aquaduct Press*, May 20, 2020) an evocative poetic sequence that is a visceral examination of dance, music, and obsession told entirely in verse. You may know Cassandra as one of our slush adventurers who can often be found helping out behind the scenes and who is also the author of *The Manticore's Vow* (*Interstellar Flight Press*, 2019).

INTERSTELLAR FLIGHT PRESS: Though the story of *Sacred Summer* is that of a woman, M., much of the action takes place in and near places dominated by men: M.'s house is built by her former husband, the women who live near her are tightly controlled by their husbands, and even the music M. finds herself again as a dancer within is written and performed by a man. Even her chosen genre of dance, ballet, is one we typically view as highly gendered.

How did the theme of gender and control drive the ways in which you crafted the poems for the book? And how do traditional tales of monsters in dark forests—generally tales that are highly gendered as well— complement and complicate the contemporary setting you use?

CASSANDRA ROSE CLARKE: *Sacred Summer* goes back to a trope I've always been fascinated by, which is the dissatisfied suburban housewife. While on the surface it's not the most relatable trope (I mean, how many of us live in designer mansions? Not me, that's for sure) it does explore themes of being isolated and imprisoned by the expectations of others. So that was my starting point with this book with regards to gender: the idea of an objectified wife who learns abruptly that her ex-husband is not terribly concerned with her as a human being, only as a muse.

As a professional ballet dancer, she is not so much an artist as an artist's medium—her body is used to express the vision of the choreographer. When she connects with the musician, their partnership is much more equal: they are each other's muses, and she draws inspiration from his music for her own art, just as he draws inspiration from her dance for his music. They are drawn together by place, by pain, by artistic obsession, and, of course, by the monster.

The monster is another complication, as she's female as well, and is an equal-opportunity terrorizer. In some ways, the musician is her Final Boy, the lone survivor of a classic horror movie plot, and the one who has to bear the suffering of being a witness. With the monster, I was really inspired by the Alien franchise, and how it pits a female hero against a female monster, and that was something I knew I wanted to do in the story as well.

IFP: The poems in this collection return again and again to consuming: the wives' consumption of Diet Coke, cigarettes, and champagne; M.'s consumption of the songs the musician creates; and ultimately, the monster's consumption of human bodies. How did you view these acts of consumption as you were writing the poems?

CRC: I think the idea of consumption strongly ties in with some of the gender stuff I was playing around with. People are so weird about women consuming anything: vices, media, food. It goes back to the core idea behind why M.'s husband asked for a divorce: She shattered the illusion that she is a work of art. Works of art don't eat lunch.

Also, with regards to the musician's songs: she's consuming a very aggressive, coded-as-masculine form of music, and I really enjoyed the contrast there, that she's finding inspiration in something loud, fast, and scream-y. One of the core images from this collection is the contrast between ballet, which in its classical form is designed to be as ethereal as possible, even as it wreaks havoc on the dancer's body, and black/death metal, which sounds and looks violent and frightening but which can't come close to the kind of actual physical damage often caused by a career in professional dance. So I felt like M's obsession with the musician's work was her way of bringing the physical pain and trauma of her chosen art form upfront.

IFP: What prompted you to write the story in a series of lyrical poems? What challenges did the form present as you were crafting the narrative? And how did the lyrical form work with (or against) the music and ballet that are so integral to the story?

CRC: To be perfectly honest, I wrote the story as a series of poems because I didn't feel like writing it as a full-on novel—I had too many other projects going on! The story came to me in fragments, and I wrote the poems out of order, one a day, as part of NaPoWriMo (National Poetry Writing Month, which happens every April and asks poets to write one poem a day for a month). Then I stitched them together to make a cohesive story.

I think the poetry format really works for this story, though, because poetry is so closely tied to music. Could it have worked as prose? Sure. But as a poetry collection, it mirrors a concept album or even a ballet: in both, individual pieces (songs, dances) are linked together to form a whole.

IFP: Are there speculative poetry collections that explore the same themes as *Sacred Summer* does that you'd like to recommend to readers of *Interstellar Flight Magazine*?

CRC: I don't know of any poetry collections offhand, unfortunately, although if anyone wants to sound off in the comments, feel free! I do want to recommend a movie that deals with a lot of these same themes, though: *Swallow*, about a woman with pica. I think it serves as a nice companion piece to *Sacred Summer*.

About the Author

Cassandra Rose Clarke's novels have been finalists for the Philip K. Dick Award, the Romantic Times Reviewer's Choice Award, and YALSA's Best Fiction for Young Adults. Her poetry has placed second in the Rhysling Awards, been nominated for the Pushcart Prize, and appeared in *Strange Horizons, Star*Line,* and elsewhere. Cassandra graduated in 2006 from The University of St. Thomas with a B.A. in English, and two years later she completed her master's degree in creative writing at The University of Texas at Austin. In 2010 she attended the Clarion West Writer's Workshop in Seattle, where she was a recipient of the Susan C. Petrey Clarion Scholarship Fund.

Bog Bodies, Moors, and Ghost Girls: An Interview with Catherine Moore, Author of Borrowings of the Shan Van Vocht

BY T.D. WALKER

"Despite what we may want to hide, the landscape holds memory."

Catherine Moore's chapbook *Borrowings of the Shan Van Vocht* (*Unsolicted Press*, April 14, 2020) explores the phenomenon of bog bodies—human cadavers mummified by peat bogs. The poems in the book are named after the bog, melting and churning, which exhumed them.

The forces of nature at work on the bog lands are also given voice in this collection—wind, sun, and the Shan Van Vocht, the bog, itself. "Shan Van Vocht" is a phonetic transliteration of the Gaelic phrase (*tSeanbhean bhocht*) for the land goddess, its meaning translates as Poor Old Woman. Interstellar Flight Mag contributor T.D. Walker sat down with Catherine Moore to discuss this evocative and haunting collection of poems.

INTERSTELLAR FLIGHT PRESS: The poems in *Borrowings of the Shan Van Vocht* give voice to bodies preserved by the bogs in which they are buried and later discovered. We hear the accounts the women and girls give of their deaths and interments in the bog, and often, these deaths are tied to beliefs about the supernatural: for example, "Auning Woman" is sacrificed to the Mother Goddess, "Camnish Woman" curses the village as her "last rites," "Drumkeeragh Woman" decries the unholy manner of her burial, among others.

And yet, you've also given us in the end notes a later view of these bodies, the evidence of their lives as collected at the time of their unearthing, so we both hear the voices and, in a sense, see what's left of their bodies.

In the first poem, "Bog Body Murmurs," the dead claim that "Our stories within the tarn are tale-less." I was also struck by the poem "Girl of the Bareler Moor," in which she claims "I have no voice in lab reports." How did the tension between the physical remains and the beliefs in the supernatural these girls and women either held or were subject to factor in your crafting the poems? Did that change over the course of writing the collection?

CATHERINE MOORE: I encountered a bog body exhibit at the National Museum in Dublin, Ireland, and I was astounded and intrigued by the details still intact. Hair, nails, and fingerprints. As I studied whorls on the hands of a bog body, as unique as my own, I asked, "Who are you?" For me, the tension between the physical remains and the spiritual being was present from the very beginning. Before I even thought about writing this collection. Back stateside, fascinated, obsessed, I delved into reading everything I could find on bog bodies. And reflecting on the sadness, many being victims of tribal sacrifice.

The research for *Borrowings of the Shan Van Vocht* came two-fold. First, there is what forensic science can tell us about the bodies, which I included in the book's endnotes. And second, I dove into relevant history to understand the sociology for each woman's time period and geography, and to inform myself on their beliefs and rituals. Studying these allowed me to inhabit the world as they might have experienced. For all the interesting insights facts may give about the re-earthed bodies, I always went back to 'who are you?' and wondered about their lives. History and forensics provided a framework for me to imagine their stories.

The bog bodies on display in museums serve as documentation of ancient violence and rituals. These ancient practices seem barbaric in modern terms, though we arguably have our own forms of barbarism. We still bury our victims within bogs, metaphorically. So, I wanted a non-judgmental tone, trying to steer the voices away from a second millennial perspective. That required many revisions to the text and an expanse of two years as I set the manuscript aside to read it again with fresh eyes. To reflect on the social and spiritual forces at play within this woman's time period and lot in life.

But the voices ended up with their own timeless commentary. When the "Girl of the Bareler Moor" says "I have no voice in lab reports," I've given her modern knowledge and fast-forwarded her voice to a contemporary setting. As one of the later poems I wrote, perhaps here I wanted a sense of endless for one struck down in short-ended youth. Also, her remains have been destroyed by modern science and I remember thinking that instead of her ancient tale, having her address a 2020 audience would bring dignity to her being.

IFP: In the collection, we hear from the women and girls whose bodies are found as well as from the wind and the sun who comment on their bodies in "The Wind Concurs" and "The Sun Questions." Why give voice to these two elements of nature?

CM: The preservation of bodies within the bogs of our Northern hemisphere relies on a unique ecosystem, so it seemed right to include natural elements in the storytelling. It was really the bog's, "Shan Van Vocht," voice that came to me first, with all its excuses and truths. Then I felt the other witnesses in this barren space should have a say—wind and sun— because despite what we may want to hide, the landscape holds memory. On my trip to Ireland, I found the expected rain and green—what I didn't anticipate was the wind. It's a windy country. Most of the island is nearly treeless, which provides a vast, wide-open space for the winds off the North Atlantic to play. Moving in rains and thwarting the sun with clouds. "The Wind Concurs" came to me in between writing the bog body poems and "The Sun Questions" inspired after. Since the bodies lay blind in muddy solitude, the elements above are the closest to providing a 'witness' or a larger point of view of the bog. If I were to re-visit the collection, I would add the voice of rain.

IFP: The chapbook ends with "Shan Van Vocht Answers," in which the voice of "Mother Nature" speaks about the process of change by noting what the bog destroys and what it leaves intact. She asserts that "I am preserving, not consuming."

The poems in *Borrowings of the Shan Van Vocht* shape a narrative about the ends of the lives of real bodies found in bogs, transforming them into a compelling whole that tells of both human cruelty and the dignity of the dead. In writing the poems for this book, did you find that your process paralleled hers, in paring away much of the story to leave your readers with those few necessary details that still speak of an entire life?

CM: As you describe it, that's a beautiful metaphor for the process of writing, particularly poetry. I hope I did justice to these deceased, in extrapolating their lives from the forensics and recorded history. The voices I created for them were based on research, reflection, and an artful listening to what we know of their life and death. I strove for homage and requiem. I often write of the nameless—like La Cueva de las Manos (Cave of Hands)— and the indelible marks they leave behind. Within *Borrowings of the Shan Van Vocht*, I intended to both unearth history and preserve it, so I suppose this makes my intentions the same as the Shan Van Vocht's.

IFP: Are there any collections that share the same themes as *Borrowings of the Shan Van Vocht* that you would like to recommend to readers of *Interstellar Flight Magazine*?

CM: Similar in approach, Louise Gluck's Pulitzer-winning collection The Wild Iris (*Ecco*, 1993) uses flowers as the voice to encompass human emotions and spiritual realms.

Of similar theme, and of noted inspiration for my collection, is famous Irish poet Seamus Heaney's bog poetry including "Bogland," "Tollund Man," and "Strange Fruit."

And the non-fiction book *Bog Bodies Uncovered: Solving Europe's Ancient Mystery* (*Thames & Hudson*, 2015) by Miranda Aldhouse-Green, explores both the science and history behind bog bodies.

About the Author

Catherine Moore is the author of three chapbooks and the collection *Ulla! Ulla!* (Main Street Rag). Her work appears in *Tahoma Literary Review, Roanoke Review, Southampton Review, Appalachian Heritage, Mid-American Review* and in various anthologies. She's been awarded Walker Percy and Hambidge fellowships and her honors include the Southeast Review's Gearhart Poetry Prize, a Nashville MetroArts grant, inclusion in the juried Best Small Fictions, as well as Pushcart and Best of the Net nominations. Catherine holds a Master of Fine Arts in Creative Writing and she teaches at a community college.

Dancing Princesses, Fairy Tales, and Portal
Fantasies: An Interview with Andrea Blythe,
author of Twelve

BY T.D. WALKER

Continuing our series of interviews with speculative poets, today T.D. Walker chats with Andrea Blythe, author of *Twelve* (*Interstellar Flight Press*, 2020). Andrea has been a regular in the speculative poetry scene for several years now, with her popular blog and a long list of outstanding poetry publications. *Twelve* is a poetic retelling of the Brothers Grimm fairytale "The Twelve Dancing Princesses." Bewitching and beguiling, this short series of linked poems takes the reader to the underground realm and back, following the stories of twelve princesses and their life after the magic shoes.

INTERSTELLAR FLIGHT PRESS: The poems in *Twelve* follow the lives of the sisters from the story "The Twelve Dancing Princesses" after their secret has been discovered, and the eldest has been married to the soldier who learned of their nightly dancing. Each sister's story tells of how she coped with the loss of the other world in which they temporarily escaped their domineering father, whose view we see in "Prelude": "Daughters were meant to be placid, pure, and idle beauties who accepted their role as tokens in the bartering of treaties."

When the twelfth sister returns to this other world which she visited last as a girl, she makes a surprising discovery upon seeing one of the fairy princes with whom she'd danced now old and wizened: "These creatures had needed them, she realized. They had drawn from the princesses some power—youth, beauty, innocence, vigor. It didn't matter what." Even in their attempts to escape from their father's dominance, it seems they are used. As the twelfth sister notes: "maybe it had always been wrong and it was only illusion that kept her sisters and her from seeing the truth beneath the pretty surface."

How did writing the poems for this collection change the way in which you read "The Twelve Dancing Princesses" now? Did that view of the story shift as you wrote about each sister? And how would you like your readers to view the original fairy tale in light of the princesses as you've rendered them?

ANDREA BLYTHE: "The Twelve Dancing Princesses" is a story that's captivated me since I was a child. I remember being enchanted by the idea of a realm under the floor, which glitters with trees made of silver, gold, and diamond—a world of magic and beauty. It has the same feel as portal fantasies, such as *The Lion, the Witch, and the Wardrobe*, which I was also fond of at the time. Sometimes the real world can feel so bland and boring when you're a kid, and I could sympathize with the desire to escape somewhere miraculous, even if that place contains dangers.

Coming back to the story decades later as an adult was interesting, in part because some of the elements in the Brothers Grimm version didn't align with the story in the way I remembered. It forced me to reconsider the story from a new perspective. In particular, I was blown away by the realization that no one in the story comes off as being particularly nice. I'm used to fairy tales taking a clear stance on such things—here's the pure, good-hearted, beautiful maiden, and here's her mean, spiteful, ugly rival. However, in "The Twelve Dancing Princesses" the lines between right and wrong are not clear.

Grey area in the moral compass of a fairy tale. How fascinating.

It was this shift in perspective that led me to begin writing the poems. In the story, the twelve sisters are presented as a single entity, acting together to drug the suitors so they can slip into the under realm for a night of dancing. Only the eldest and youngest sisters speak or show agency outside of the group—the eldest delivering the cup of drugged wine to the suitor and the youngest expressing fears about being caught out.

Writing these poems allowed me to consider these women as individuals. Once the dancing is taken from them, each of the sisters begin to explore their own individual desires and claim them. As I explored the different possibilities of their choices, I learned more about what kind of women they could have been.

IFP: In the author's note, you mention your appreciation for fairy tales, even as you didn't subscribe to their messages. You also give us background about the story in its various versions and how you researched not only the story itself but also how it fails to fit neatly into a typical fairy tale structure. Did you do research for the individual poems? If so, how did that shape the way you saw the sisters as individuals and as a unit?

AB: A lot of my research began with trying to understand why the ending I read in the Brothers Grimm version of the story didn't align with a version I read as a child, which I could not find. (In the Brothers Grimm, the eldest princess is selected as the bride, while in the version I remembered, it was the youngest.) While I was digging into the different versions—and failing to find the story I remembered—I learned more about "The Twelve Dancing Princesses." It brought an immediacy to the story to the extent that I couldn't stop thinking about it, which ultimately brought me to writing these poems.

However, most of my writing process is instinctual, particularly in the initial drafts. I tend to catch upon an image that compels me and use it as a kicking off point to discover the poem, drawing on things I've read over the years about folklore or alchemy. My process for *Twelve* was similar. After writing the eldest sister and exploring her white-hot rage, I knew I wanted to consider how each of the other sisters would react when the dancing comes to an end. While some, like the eldest, would be angry, others might be anxious, thrilled, or relieved.

Some research came into play when I started to dig deeper into the editing process and wanted to clarify the details. For example, with the eldest sister, I went down a rabbit hole figuring out what kinds of old-fashioned poisons someone might slip into another person's food, particularly ones based on plants. This led me to wonder where she might be getting these plants—the answer being from one of her sisters, who would be using them for an entirely different purpose. That purpose was alchemy, which I had read about extensively in the past. Though, I did some searching to make sure I had the terminology right.

IFP: The poem that struck me most is that of "The Eighth and Ninth Sisters," who cut off their hair, wear men's clothing, and strike out to live a life of infamy as "The Black Fox," a figure of legend who is part highwayman, part hero. The pair engage in the most masculine form of rebellion, but you've undercut this with their cooperation, which we see more often in tales about women working together to overcome some plight.

What was it about a legend of someone who cannot be defined that drew you to place these sisters within it? And how do you view them in light of "The Eleventh Sister," who goes in search of the old woman who defied the principle that "women kept each other's secrets" and who thus betrayed them to the soldier and their father?

AB: Thank you for that. "The Eighth and Ninth Sisters" is one of my personal favorites as well. My vision for The Black Fox was inspired by legendary figures, such as Zorro, Robin Hood, the Man in Black in *The Princess Bride*, or the Bluejay in Cornelia Funke's *Inkspell*. Much like fairy tales, these kinds of legendary outlaw heroes often have legends grow up around them, causing their story to change shape depending on who is doing the telling. Growing up, I remember being captivated by such figures. I wanted to be the outlaw, the one who dons a mask, leaps into epic sword fights, and fights for justice outside of the law.

As I was working through *Twelve*, I knew that I wanted to include at least one pair of twins and the idea that they would become The Black Fox came quickly after (the name partly drawn from the "Mr. Fox" fairy tale). Twins, in general, are often treated as a single unit—and I was interested in the idea of a legend growing around them, a story so strong that it turns two women into a single outlaw. The legend defines them, but also sets them free to be any version of The Black Fox they want to be.

Before your question, I had not considered "The Eleventh Sister" in relation to the "The Eighth and Ninth Sisters." When I think about it though, the eleventh sister's search for the old woman is tied to this aspect of legend-making. Old women are found throughout fairy tales, sometimes taking the role of the witch, sometimes the helpful old lady. They rarely have names, and as such, they could almost all be the same old woman, providing help or retribution as they see fit.

For the eleventh sister, the old woman is a figure of betrayal and a mystery. Who is she? And how could she reveal her sisters' secret? As she continues searching for the old woman, the woman grows into a deeper legend for her and the more she herself becomes wrapped up in that legend—until she not only can't escape it, but becomes a part of it.

IFP: Are there speculative poetry collections that explore the same themes as *Twelve* does that you'd like to recommend to readers of Interstellar Flight Magazine?

AB: If you're wanting to be introduced to a multitude of amazing feminist poetry all at once, I recommend picking up *Moment of Change* (*Aqueduct Press*, 2012), an anthology of feminist speculative poetry edited by R.B. Lemberg. It showcases tons of amazing work from a multitude of great poets.

Another feminist spin on fairy tales is Anne Sexton's *Transformations* (*Mariner Books*, 2001), which I read years ago and was a great inspiration for how I approach retellings. Her poems put new spins on the classic tales in a way that still feels intimately connected to the original.

More on the science fiction side, I'd highly recommend *Soft Science* (*Alice James Books*, 2019) by Franny Choi, in which she explores her explores queer, Asian American femininity through the lens of robots, cyborgs, and artificial intelligence.

Twelve: Poems Inspired by the Brothers Grimm Fairy Tale is Interstellar Flight Press' first poetry chapbook by Andrea Blythe. It's available for purchase now.

About the Author

Andrea Blythe bides her time waiting for the apocalypse by writing speculative poetry and fiction. She is the author of *Your Molten Heart / A Seed to Hatch* (2018) a collection of erasure poems created from the pages of Trader Joe's Fearless Flyers, and coauthor of *Every Girl Becomes the Wolf* (*Finishing Line Press*, 2018), a collaborative chapbook written with

Laura Madeline Wiseman. She is a cohost of the New Books in Poetry podcast and is a member of the Science Fiction and Fantasy Poetry Association and the Horror Writers Association. Find her on Twitter or at www.andreablythe.com.

#NotAllHeroes: An Interview with Tochi Onyebuchi, Author of Riot Baby

BY JAMILEH JEMISON

"It's so multiform, this confluence of race and violence. I mean, that's the American story. The intended extermination of indigenous peoples to clear land for white colonizers, slavery, Redemption and the birth of the KKK, Japanese internment camps, the economic violence that persists to this day regarding mainland governmental and financial relations with Puerto Rico, those are all rib bones connected to the narrative vector of white supremacy in America." —Tochi Onyebuchi

*R*iot Baby (*Tor Books*, 2020) is a poetic, time-telescoping, dodgeball hit of a novella, by Tochi Onyebuchi, Nommo Award winning author of *Beasts Made of Night* (*Razorbill*, 2017), *Crown of Thunder* (*Razorbill*, 2018), and *War Girls* (*Razorbill*, 2019). The polymath New England native and keen cultural observer shared some thoughts about the narrators Ella and Kev and what informed his latest work.

INTERSTELLAR FLIGHT PRESS: What was energizing and what was challenging about writing a book of this length?

TOCHI ONYEBUCHI: The novella format has enjoyed such a thrilling resurgence over the past decade, and it has been so heartening to watch. As its own format, it doesn't feel like a "slim novel" or a too-long short story. You can do an immense amount of worldbuilding, but it all needs to matter in a more urgent way than if you're afforded the sprawl of a novel. So, concision and writing-by-implication, figuring out how to do those things, was immensely energizing. It felt like I'd developed a new master of my One-For-All Quirk like Midoriya in Season 2 of My Hero Academia.

The biggest challenge was keeping the focus tight. There were so many directions the story could have spiraled out into, so many different paths to take, and I wanted and felt empowered to take all of them, but it would have left the novella overheated.

IFP: How did you create the feeling of physical and temporal vastness in such a short book?

TO: I needed to make sure Ella's powers were in service of the story. That meant not just having her struggle with them in the mold of a traditional Western narrative arc, but also using them to make the points I wanted to make, namely about the vast continuum of (state-sanctioned) white violence historically visited on Black Americans.

Speculative fiction afforded me the tools to literalize the exploration of that continuum, to render the experience of it tactile and immediate in the prose. What might have been a multi-generational, 500-page tome wrapped around these thematic vertebrae can then be compressed to fewer than 200 pages.

What writing with these supernatural powers allowed me to do was basically to translocate experience. As far as the traveling across time, I might have had some of Paul Harding's *Tinkers* (*Bellevue Literary Press*, 2019) in the back of my head; so much is done with so little space. But I wanted to layer onto that so that it's not just the reader experiencing those time jumps, it's the characters too.

IFP: I'm very interested in the use of names in Riot Baby: who has them, who doesn't, and when. There's a rhythm of many named characters in the first beats of the story then far fewer until the last chapter of the book. Can you share your thoughts on the meaning of names and naming in the book?

TO: That's a very interesting question. I think this is one of those instances where my decision-making was guided more by intuition than by conscious thought. And intuition, while writing, is one of the ways in which rhythm establishes itself. Often, for me, recurring characters are the most likely to be named (and their status might change from draft to draft though they keep the name), but another thing at work is that, as the book progresses, Ella spends more and more time looking at the past. And even though the experiences for her are immediate, by virtue of her abilities, there's still a remove. She has the moment, but she doesn't always necessarily have the life leading up to that moment, so to speak.

So, I think those two things—whether or not a character was recurring and the distance that persists despite the bridging of a gap of history—powered my naming logic. Another thing at work within Ella, too, was a genre of the same feeling I felt by, I think, 2016 when the names of so many African Americans had been emblazoned as hashtags after their deaths at the hands of police that a sort of profane amalgamation started to occur. "Oh, are you going to the protest? For the boy who got shot by police. No, the other one. No, the other other one." There's so much of it that the individual vessel of a soul is obliterated and what remains is the anger-grief that glows in the left-behind.

IFP: Riot Baby speaks to multiple cultural continuums around race, violence, and how both of those get systematized into whatever technology is current. It also lays out a world and characters containing multitudes. Is it appealing to you to explore this continuum more in your own writing?

TO: Back in 2016, I watched the docuseries *OJ: Made in America* (ESPN). Using OJ Simpson's football career, post-football life, and trial as a prism, it turned race relations in the US into the stuff of Greek tragedy. I felt at times, watching OJ go from black football star on USC's lily-white college campus to what he becomes before and over the course of the trial, and the word Aeschylean kept coming to mind. It spun out from his story to create this vast picture of being black in modern America, and it convinced me that the most compelling narrative vector in the story of America is race.

It's so multiform, this confluence of race and violence. I mean, that's the American story. The intended extermination of indigenous peoples to clear land for white colonizers, slavery, Redemption and the birth of the KKK, Japanese internment camps, the economic violence that persists to this day regarding mainland governmental and financial relations with Puerto Rico, those are all rib bones connected to the narrative vector of white supremacy in America.

One of the most fascinating periods of American history to me is Reconstruction where you get these inklings of what this country might look like were a spirit of racial reconciliation actually worked towards, one of the greatest experiments in democratic governance. And you have things like the South Carolina constitution of 1868 which was drafted by recently emancipated poor, illiterate men and women and it guaranteed public education and female suffrage as well as abolishing race discrimination. Then "economically anxious" whites obliterated it all.

All of which is to say that there's a hell of a lot of story there.

IFP: Can you talk about what the n-word means to Kev and how he uses it?

TO: For him, it's a sort of signaling. A way of acknowledging sameness with others like him, whether that sameness is their incarceration, their post-incarceration, their unofficial status as boys-outside-the-bodega, or what have you. It also, at a certain point, becomes a grammatical quirk, like a comma or exclamation point. Or, perhaps more appropriately, a bit of musical notation. A caesura or quarter tone that can alter, tonally, the meaning of a whole sentence.

IFP: You've asked readers to reflect on the last word of the book and whether its meaning to them is likely the same as its meaning to others. What kinds of responses have you had to this?

TO: I'm not privy to the race of most reviewers who've written about the book, and so far, many of them have written glowingly about it, for which I'm immensely grateful. But, given demographic totals in the publishing industry, I don't think it's a stretch to say that, statistically, the book is reaching many white interrogators and commentators within the literary ecosystem. And many, many of them have called the ending "hopeful," which is, so far, a source of endless fascination for me.

I'm reminded of the reaction to *Get Out* (*Blumhouse*, 2017) and how many young whites either couldn't or wouldn't relate to or see themselves in Allison Williams's character. Or they would try to justify her character's actions when she was an actual white supremacist who ate cereal with the Fruit Loops and the milk separately. All of which is to say that *Riot Baby* ends in a conflagration. And I'll always be wondering who reads the book and doesn't see themselves trapped in the fire. And who does.

IFP: I am also a lifetime New Englander and have a deep affection for our varied region-specific attractions—Mark Twain House, Bridge of Flowers, coffee milk, etc. What are some of your favorite regional oddities/delights?

TO: To be honest, so much of the region, connected as it is with my memories of an idyllic childhood and blue-collar adolescence, feels to me like a dreamscape. My appreciation of the region stems from the moments it gave me.

The Christmas cantata at our old Colonial Congregationalist church where the centerpiece performance of "O, Holy Night" was a reminder of what mercy sounded like. Or being out late in early February shoveling a driveway as the snow's still coming down, but it's sucked up all the sound around you so that you work in silence while your mother sleeps before preparing for a morning shift at the hospital.

In the town where I came of age, our downtown is a single intersection, and when a Starbucks first moved in, it was a very big deal. But the public library is within walking distance from our house, and during that point in the fall when the leaves are carmine and the sky is that graying shade of blue and some of the sidewalks are covered in pine needles and you have to tuck your chin into your scarf while the wind bites at your cheeks, and maybe there's a loved one on your arm or maybe you're ambling alone but finally able to hear your own thoughts, that walk can give you the most sublime minutes of your day.

Riot Baby kicks off in a near-history Los Angeles set to boil, a sharp contrast to the current New England winter, or a familiar bass line under our complicated present. Best devoured whole, make a pact with a friend to read it one weekend so you have someone to discuss it with. *Riot Baby* and Tochi Onyebuchi's other speculative novels can be found wherever books are sold.

About the Author

Tochi Onyebuchi graduated from Yale University, New York University's Tisch School of the Arts, Columbia Law School, and L'institut d'études politiques with a Masters degree in Global Business Law. His short fiction has appeared in *Asimov's Science Fiction, Omenana, Black Enough: Stories of Being Young & Black in America*, and elsewhere. His non-fiction has appeared in *Uncanny Magazine, Nowhere Magazine*, Tor.com and the Harvard Journal of African-American Public Policy.

No Polar Bears in the Antarctic But Plenty of Women in Space: An Interview with Laura Lam, author of Goldilocks

BY JT MORSE

"Earth spread below them, sunset deepening back to night. They were over Asia—there was the little finger of Japan and Korea, the sprawl of China. Shocks of light from Tokyo, Beijing, Seoul. The cities were bigger, buildings for accommodation and business, but also vertical farms. Sea walls protected the changed coastline as best they could, and more walls bisected landmasses in a futile attempt to stop the next wave of climate change refugees who had nowhere else to go. So many millions of people far below them. If the *Atalanta* didn't make it, all those lights would darken." —Excerpt from Goldilocks by Laura Lam (*Orbit*, May 5, 2020)

From *Vestigial Tales* (*Penglass Publishing*, 2014) to *Dark World* to *Pantomime* (*Pan*, 2015) and *Shadow Play* (*Pan*, 2015), Laura Lam has been hard at work for years, blowing spec fic readers' minds. This California transplant, now living in Scotland, also writes F/F romance as Laura Ambrose. Interstellar Flight Magazine contributor J.T. Morse had the pleasure of recently digging into what makes her literary clock tick.

INTERSTELLAR FLIGHT PRESS: Every writer needs the right place in which to cultivate their creative whims and genius; your shift from sunny California to cloudy Scotland seems to be working for you in that vein. What drew you to Scotland, and are there any particular aspects of the culture or landscape that inspire your literary creations?

LAURA LAM: I met a boy on the internet when I was 15 and he was 16, back in 2003. We were friends for a year and then dated long-distance for five years—I'd come to Scotland every summer and some winters—and then I moved in 2009 after I finished university. So it's his fault, but I love Scotland—the moody weather, the people, the twisty wynds of Edinburgh, the dramatic landscape of the Highlands and the Islands. I haven't written that much directly about Scotland yet, though she does creep in around the corners. There's a scene in *Goldilocks* set in Sutherland, where they may or may not build a spaceport on the A' Mhòine peninsula.

IFP: Although you have a handful of romance books published under the pen name "Laura Ambrose," being a magazine catering more to spec fic lovers and literature, we think our readership will be most interested in your science fiction, space opera, and fantasy works. But before we trek down that genre fork in the path, we'd love to know how you juggle the realms of romance and spec fic? Are there ever times when your genre-children compete with one another or are you one big happily balanced, multi-genre family most of the time?

LL: I had a gap in Laura Lam releases, and I thought it would be fun to release some F/F romance novellas set in geeky settings like SFF conventions (*A Hidden Hope, Penglass Publishing*, 2018), an SFF publisher (*A Perfect Balance, Penglass Publishing*, 2018), and starring an SFF writer with writer's block (*An Unheard Song, Penglass Publishing*, 2019). They're lighthearted and sweet, and they were a nice change of pace. I've only released 3, and I'm not releasing any in 2020, but if there are no Laura Lam releases in 2021 (depending on publisher schedules), I might put out some more. I like keeping my hand in self-publishing as I feel I learn a few more things each time I do it. The romances are more of a hobby at present—they've made me some pocket change, but to be successful at self-pub I'd likely have to publish a novella every other month and devote a lot more time to marketing, and between the SFF and my day job as a lecturer, I just can't balance all 3, sadly. I read across all genres and would happily write across them too, but my heart always lies with SFF.

IFP: Let's dive into your latest release, ***Goldilocks***, for a few questions. First, hit us with a brief plot summary and the publication details.

LL: *Goldilocks* is about the first all-female space mission to an exosolar planet called Cavendish, 10.5 light years away. It's humanity's last hope, as Earth only has 30 years left of habitability thanks to climate change and overpopulation. Yet at the last minute, the women were kicked off of the mission through a loophole, and NASA planned to send 5 men instead. The women knew they were the best people suited to the mission, so they stole the spaceship and headed off anyway. Yet there are secrets on board that could threaten to undo everything they've worked for. It's out in the UK on April 30th through Wildfire/Headline and May 5th through Orbit.

IFP: We've got the *Goldilocks* basics, now give us the dirt. Something nitty-gritty, hush-hush, or never-before-revealed. Maybe a funny anecdote about how this story came to you, a scandalous typo in a promotional image, or anything out of the ordinary.

LL: For quite a few drafts, I kept saying there were polar bears in the Antarctic, which is just not true. As well, the book came about through a weird series of coincidences after chatting with Alex Clarke, editor of Wildfire, at the Edinburgh Bookshop. I sold it on a two-chapter partial, which is a first for me. It meant I had to write the rest of the book in about six months.

IFP: Fun facts! Who knew about those imaginary polar bears in Antarctica? Thanks for opening up to us, Laura. Last *Goldilocks*-related question. How did it feel to see one of your books turned into a promotional trailer, and what was your level of involvement in the process?

LL: It was very cool! I'd never had a book trailer before, and it feels very cinematic and epic. I wasn't involved at all—it was all the marketer, Joe Yule. He was the one who came up with putting in the snow globe, which ends up being thematically relevant.

IFP: Let's talk sci-fi/fantasy influences and loves. Which authors have most influenced your SFF writing, and what books are you reading right now, or have read recently, that you'd recommend for spec fic readers?

LL: In fantasy, Robin Hobb, Scott Lynch, and more recently Zen Cho and N.K. Jemsin are top faves. In SF, Becky Chambers, some of Alfred Bester's work, and Octavia Butler. Right now I'm reading Neil Gaiman's *Norse Mythology* (*W.W. Norton & Co*, 2017) in hardback and re-listening to *Fool's Errand* by Robin Hobb on audio book. I finished *Wanderers* (*Del Ray*, 2019) by Chuck Wendig not long ago, which is good but incredibly relevant. I had to take a break and read a rom-com at one point in the second half.

Well, there you have it folks, the need-to-knows about Laura Lam, *Goldilocks*, women in space, and polar bears that may or may not be living the Antarctic.
About the Author

Laura Lam's other works include the feminist space opera *Seven Devils* (co-written with Elizabeth May), BBC Radio 2 Book Club section *False Hearts*, the companion novel *Shattered Minds*, and the award-winning Micah Grey series: *Pantomime*, *Shadowplay*, and *Masquerade*. She lectures part-time at Edinburgh Napier University on the Creative Writing MA. For the latest information about Laura and her literary ventures, you can visit her website or reach out to her on Twitter or Instagram at @LR_Lam.

One Song to Ruin Us All (in a Good Way): Interview with LGBTQ+ Romantic Fantasy Author Julia Ember

BY JT MORSE

"Writing retellings is a lot like writing historical fiction in a way, in that you have an existing cast, some story beats, and myths that lots of people know."
—Julia Ember

There are many things to be thankful for in 2020; one of the most exciting for writer Julia Ember was the release of her latest book *Ruinsong (Farrar, Straus and Giroux,* 2020). *Ruinsong* is a dark and lush LGBTQ+ romantic fantasy about two young women from rival factions that must work together to reunite their country as they wrestle with their feelings for each other. To learn more about this exciting new novel and its amazing author, enjoy this interview with Julia Ember.

INTERSTELLAR FLIGHT PRESS: Seeing as *The Seafarer's Kiss (Interlude Press,* 2017) is based on the story of the classic fairytale by Hans Christian Andersen, *The Little Mermaid* and *Ruinsong* is a reimagining of Gaston Leroux's *The Phantom of the Opera,* when did you first come up with the idea or discover your passion for retelling classic tales?

JULIA EMBER: It sort of happened by accident, initially! When I wrote *The Seafarer's Kiss,* I had just left graduate school and was weighing up what I wanted to do with my life since I had decided I didn't want to become an academic. I studied Medieval Literature and History in graduate school, and outside of teaching, there isn't much you can do with that. So, I started writing again in this interim period of figuring things out and decided I wanted to write a mermaid story. The idea to do a Viking retelling of *The Little Mermaid* was my way of trying to incorporate some of what I'd studied into a new passion.

IFP: I can imagine that, as with all writing, there are benefits and drawbacks to this "retelling" style of storytelling. Could you give us some insights into the challenges and perks you've encountered while penning stories based on classic tales?

JE: I think the major perk is that you have a jumping-off point. Writing retellings is a lot like writing historical fiction in a way, in that you have an existing cast, some story beats, and myths that lots of people know. However, on the flip side, people have strong attachments to the classics and strong opinions on what a retelling should look like. My stories don't tend to follow the original super closely—the settings are often vastly different, they're queer, and incorporate magic. Some readers love that departure, but you do get other readers who are upset that the elements they loved most in the original tale might not present in your retelling.

IFP: Without further ado, tell us some of the who, what, when, and where of your exciting new release, *Ruinsong*.

JE: *Ruinsong* is a high fantasy retelling of *The Phantom of the Opera*, set in a world where magic is sung. It follows two protagonists from rival, warring factions. Cadence, a powerful mage, has become the tool of the country's tyrant queen, using her magic to subdue the rebelling nobility. Remi is the daughter of a viscount, with allegiances to the rebellion. The two girls were friends as young children, before the queen's brutal reign tore the country apart. When they are thrust back together, Cadence has to make a choice: use her powerful voice for good and fight with the rebellion or follow in the queen's brutal footsteps.

IFP: Okay, let's get personal. Seventy countries?! How have you visited that many countries in your relatively short lifespan and why? Also, would you say all the travel has done more to help or hinder your writing/career?

JE: Both of my parents have a lot of wanderlust! They moved us to England when I was nine, and we traveled somewhere during every school break. My dad had a mission—now exceeded—to visit one hundred countries himself, so he was always looking for somewhere new! That travel bug has rubbed off on me, and I've continued to travel whenever I can. Being in new places really refills my creative well, so I would say it helps my writing. It's been hard this year with Covid because we haven't gone anywhere, and I can tell that staying at home all the time has really depleted my stores of creative energy.

IFP: Pets, often an author's best frenemy—sometimes an inspiration to the work and at others an absolute distraction and detriment. Tell us about your menagerie and which one, or ones, might be your muse(s) in flesh.

JE: At the time of writing, I currently have two cats, a horse, and a ball python. I'm hoping to add another horse and a dog next year though, so the menagerie is growing! Much like travel, I find riding horses really inspiring and refreshing creatively. There's something really magical about exploring the woods or the highlands with just a horse for company. As for my cats ... I wouldn't call them muses! More like perpetual distractions, but I do love them.

IFP: Give us three adjectives to describe your style of writing and three adjectives that encompass you as a writer. Go.

JE: Intricate, character-driven, lush. Anxious hot mess! (Partially kidding, but not really.)

IFP: Final inquiries: Where can we stalk you online and where are your books currently being sold?

JE: You can order signed copies of any of my books from my local independent bookstore, Third Place Books. Copies can also be ordered through pretty much any bookstore. You can find me on Instagram at @juliaemberya or on Twitter as @jules_chronicle!

A huge thank you to Julia for taking the time to share this great book release news and tidbits about herself with our Interstellar Flight Magazine readership. Until next time, this is JT Morse saying, "Stay weird, consume copious amounts of spec fic, and pardon as many turkeys as you can; 2020's been hard on all of us."

About the Author

Julia Ember is the author of *The Seafarer's Kiss* duology and *Ruinsong*. Her work has been featured in USA Today, Bustle, Book Riot, and Autostraddle, among many other prominent outlets. Julia has a lifelong appreciation for history and classic literature and holds an MLitt in Medieval Literature from the University of St. Andrews. She currently lives in Seattle with her wife and two very fluffy cats.

Slashers, Carnivals, & Urban Legends: An Interview with Jessica Guess, Author of Cirque Berserk

BY VANESSA MAKI

"Black women and girls can literally be anything they want and I'm not just talking about the positive things. Yeah, yeah, you can be a doctor or lawyer or whatever, but you also have a right to the rage you feel inside. You have a right to be angry. You can indulge in that anger. You don't have to be this self-sacrificing trope or emotional dumping ground that the world wants you to be." —Jessica Guess

Cirque Berserk (*Unnerving*, 2020), a horror novella released this year by author Jessica Guess, is a slasher treat for horror fans. It follows main character Rochelle and a group of her friends who use their senior trip to visit the abandoned carnival Cirque Berserk. What is presumed to be an urban legend turns into an adventure filled with bloodshed, betrayal, and insanity. A trip that should have been fun becomes a nightmare that some may not survive. IFP's Vanessa Maki sat down with Guess to discuss how to come up with characters, writing tension in horror, and her fav slasher flicks.

INTERSTELLAR FLIGHT PRESS: What a pleasure it was to read Cirque Berserk and mark this as my first interview for Interstellar Flight Press. Do you mind sharing how this book came to be?

JESSICA GUESS: The premise itself started with a character. I had this image in my head of someone doing something horrific while Rhythm of the

Night by Debarge played in the

background. The image was so strange and fantastic that I had to write it. I had to put together why this person was doing this bad thing and the idea of the carnival was the only logical place to me. Then early in the brainstorming process, I saw the Rewind or Die call for novel submissions and I worked out the time and framing devices and there it was.

IFP: Having Rochelle be a Black girl and a vital part of this book lends

something new to horror. Especially in terms of her being an antagonist and leaning into tropes for manipulative purposes. What do you want black readers of Cirque Berserk to take away from her character, if anything?

JG: That Black women and girls can literally be anything they want and I'm not just talking about the positive things. Yeah, yeah, you can be a doctor or lawyer or whatever, but you also have a right to the rage you feel inside. You have a right to be angry. You can indulge in that anger. You don't have to be this self-sacrificing trope or emotional dumping ground that the world wants you to be. You can want things. Bad things if you so choose.

IFP: Writing horror novels can be a challenge because of how difficult

it can be to write believable tension and fear, though you successfully achieved that with Cirque Berserk. Were you worried about the tension not landing throughout the story?

JG: Honestly, no. Tension is my thing. I did a whole project/lesson on it in grad school. It's my jam. My concerns were more that people wouldn't get it. They wouldn't get Rochelle's rage or her actions. I was afraid they wouldn't stay with the story until a certain scene happens because that scene is when everything [in the novel] changes. Up until that scene, the reader thinks they know what this is all about. They think they know how this will go. After that scene is when all the fun starts. But I think I put enough fun stuff in there to keep the reader's attention.

IFP: Were you inspired by any other horror works (whether they be movies, TV, other books etcetera)? It's got a very '80s vibe, despite it being primarily set in 2019.

JG: The 80s were the golden era of slashers, and Cirque Berserk is a homage to that era. As for the influences, yeah, *A Nightmare on Elm Street* is definitely an influence in that I wanted a fun slasher. *Scream* and *Urban Legend* are also strong influences because they are aware of the genre. *Scream* knows all the tropes of a slasher and talks about them and *Urban Legend* had some of the best kill scenes I've ever seen so they were in the back of my head when I was writing it. I'd also have to say *Psycho* and *Death Proof* because of what those movies do with POV. In both of those movies, you think you're following one person/group of people, but then something happens and then you realize that they weren't the main attraction, so to speak.

IFP: Cirque Berserk is certainly written in a way that could be adapted into film. If you were able to make that happen—what would that look like for you?

JG: Well, for one, Tabitha Brown's daughter, Choyce Brown, would play Rochelle. I don't know if she acts at all, but I saw her doing a modeling shoot on Instagram and I was shocked because it was like Rochelle walked out of my head and into the real world. I don't even know if she's into horror or would be the least bit interested, but if she was and I could have my dream cast, it'd be her. I'd want it to have an 80s and 90s slasher vibe to it. I picture bright colors and powerful imagery.

IFP: Do you currently have any other horror projects in the works? If so, anything you'd like to or can share?

JG: A short story of mine is in season 2 of Tor Nightfire's audio horror anthology *Come Join Us by the Fire*. It's titled "Mama Tulu" and it's available for free on Google Play. I also have a short story called "The Nightmare Man" coming out in January 2021 as a part of the *Shiver Anthology* that author Nico Bell put together. Right now, I'm focusing on teaching, but I have an idea for a novella that I want to get started on soon.

About the Author

Jessica Guess is a writer and English teacher who hails from Fort Lauderdale, Florida. She earned her Creative Writing MFA from Minnesota State University, Mankato in 2018 and is the founder of the website Black Girl's Guide to Horror where she examines horror movies in terms of quality and intersectionality.

2020 Alternate Endings

FLASH FICTION

2020 Alternate Endings

I n 2020, we asked writers to reimagine our world for the better. Our guest editor chose to highlight BIPOC Black, Indigenous, and people of color writers who re-envision the future. We also raised funds from donations for the Black Lives Matter movement.

What were you imagining for 2020 when it began? It was a unique, hard, and strange year, one in which apocalypse bingo was a monthly occurrence. We asked authors: Does it feel like tempting fate too much to ask if our current reality can get any worse OR any better? We invited writers to fast forward and tell us how any or all of 2020's chaotic plot lines resolve, get tangled, tied off, or cut. Does the fae spell break at 00:00:01 on Jan 1, 2021? Is a free-roaming space colony in Andromeda still trying to wipe out a sentient mutated Covid-19 200 years from now? They showed us our futures in evocative, speculative flash fiction that responds to what humanity is facing this year. These are our alternate endings.

Our Guest Editor for this call was Jamileh Jemison.

BY JAMILEH JEMISON

Do you remember it, the weight of the early pandemic? Uncertainty like a second skin, living in a time loop, niggling doubts growing into chatty apparitions. And the violence. By the end of May 2020 police had killed 510 Americans, almost one third of them were black[1],[2]. That was the frothing cauldron that bought forth the 2020 Alternate Endings call for submissions: to feature and amplify the voices of Global Majority writers; asking them to imagine how we might emerge from all this human-wrought horror, for better and for worse.

We received over 50 stories. The seven selected map futures for us in action, mystery, humor, and poetry. Gods, time travelers, some local aliens, and innovative scientists all try their hand at a solution.

It takes a village to publish a story, the pulsing heart of IFP is our diverse crew of slush adventurers who help us pare a whole vat of stories to a long list. Luckily, the heartbreak of narrowing the list to seven is healed by the joy of working closely with the selected writers. Writing short is less forgiving than writing long; and coaxing a story out of its bud to full flower is a complex negotiation between the words, structure, and the writers' and editor's visions. That practice was a pleasure with Andrea Kriz, Suhaila Sundararajan, Natachi Mez, Archita Mittra, Nisola Jegede, Justin C. Key, Tlotlo Tsamaase, who produced gorgeous work and on deadline! Their stars are already rising, so peep their other work. Thank you all for fulling this call with such heart and imagination.

As I write this note, it is the 50th anniversary of Marvin Gaye's timeless album What's Going On? and days away from the one-year anniversary of George Floyd's murder. There are fewer police-involved deaths than this time last year, the World Health Organization recognizes five vaccines[3] to protect against the COVID-19 virus, an accomplished Global Majority woman is Vice President of the United States. It feels like our own alternate ending to 2020 is emerging.

Maybe it's cheesy, but I've always believed dreaming is the first step toward the next great thing. Want a better world? Get as many people dreaming one up as possible! The stories we tell give those dreams voice, and when we all raise our voices, we drive change. We need your voice too. Read these dreamers, get inspired and keep writing.

—Jamileh Jemison

---

1. https://mappingpoliceviolence.org/ - accessed 22 May 2020
2. https://www.cbsnews.com/pictures/black-people-killed-by-police-in-the-u-s-in-2020/84/ - accessed 22 May 2020
3. https://www.who.int/groups/strategic-advisory-group-of-experts-on-immunization/covid-19-materials - accessed 22 May 2020

For You, 2000 Quarantines From Now

BY ANDREA KRIZ

I peered through the lens and jerked back, my eyes seared by fluorescent green. *Finally.* Seven years of thesis research had yielded this—a mixture of RNA and protein that had eliminated SARS-CoV20XX from every cell in the dish. I'd almost lost hope. Lifeline had taken to the skies, vowing to end the ground world pandemics before COVID-2100. The Conductor had kept the promise, technically. The trainship's holo-notebooks had been frozen on 20XX for decades before I'd even come up here. As I logged my results, the walls rattled. Turbulence, I thought, until I realized: the comforting shake and rumble of my labcube—of Lifeline itself—had actually stopped. Unnerved, I grabbed a tube of sample and poked my head out of my microscope module.

"What's—?"

A spike burst through the ceiling, skimming my cheek. Seven more followed suit, crashing around me in a cage. Lights pressed down on me. The feathery brush of needles next. They inched toward the tube clenched in my fist.

"Get down!"

I hugged the floor just in time for a gunshot to nearly take out my hearing. The pipettor thrashed—and went dark, smoking from a bullet hole inches from my face. Through the half-collapsed ceiling, I saw a figure made tall with synthetics. 2S, her oil-splattered badge projected. One of the myriad security guards that patrolled the hidden corridors of Lifeline.

"Congrats, kid. You must've found it."

"What?"

"The vaccine."

I didn't correct her. Seas of shards littered the floor. 2S and the pipettor's scuffle had shattered the flasks that held my samples. She only had eyes for the tube in my fist as she grabbed my arm, pulling me up through the remains of the ceiling. Her grip was cold metal, like the pistol she clutched in her other hand. Still, my heart pounded at the contact. As soon as I found my footing I tore away, putting the mandated six feet between us. We were in the labcube above mine. Also littered with sparking carcasses—2S's work. A honeycomb of the same one-person lab spaces loomed above us, through webs of collapsed beams. My mouth hung open. But that was nothing compared to what awaited us —

Outside.

Freezing wind whipped my face as I followed 2S through the rubble, up to a jagged breach in the side of the car itself. I'd last seen Lifeline's hull on the ground world, as a child. A leviathan of steel and steam that had descended from the skies and hovered over our quarantine bunker, dispensing antibody scans, aptitude tests, and a way out for a handful of kids—myself included. I barely recognized its snowy, rusted surface now. As we floated over the mountainside below, our car's shadow *moved*. A swarm of the same machines that had attacked me.

"More pipettors?!"

Self-assembling robots designed to do lab work remotely after researchers went into the first quarantine. The reason Lifeline had taken to the skies. On the ground world, they became autonomous enough to figure out what vaccine development actually entailed—and didn't like the idea of becoming obsolete.

"How'd they get up here?"

"Raiders bring 'em," 2S growled. "Use the buggers' networks to track down researchers close to a breakthrough and crack the hull. Then they swoop in."

"Raiders?"

A draconic shape broke through the clouds, clawing rivulets down Lifeline's side as it landed. I fought the urge to run toward it. These beasts, reverse-engineered from dinosaur DNA to fight the pipettors, had been the superheroes of my childhood. I'd spent countless afternoons watching them patrol the skies above our bunker. But this one glared at me through an eye crisscrossed with scars.

"That's the vaccine, right?" its rider barked. "Give it to me."

He wore scrap, spray-painted lurid pink and green, but I could still make out the numbers of the Lifeline car it'd been stripped from.

"You Lifeliners owe it to us. For abandoning us."

"I didn't mean to—"

The raider lunged for my tube. 2S fired. The sky rumbled. And it began to snow. The draconid screeched as a flake hit its eye, careening backward. 2S tackled me out of the way and they went over the edge. Their choking rang in my ears long after they were gone.

"Careful," 2S panted. "Not. Normal snow. Viralfall."

She hunched over me, blocking the flakes with her body. Lifeline shook beneath us. I followed 2S's gaze and saw a gangway extending from the neighboring car.

"Go."

"What about you?"

"Don't worry. I'm resistant." She tapped her neck; metal rang. "Synthetic respiratory system. I'll follow after I disconnect this car."

"Disconnect?"

"We saved what we could. Gotta keep Lifeline moving."

The gangway shuddered to a stop at my feet. I made out sleek instruments in the hallway beyond—and realized everything in my labcube had been battered hand-me-downs. I'd never thought of the *rest* of Lifeline. Not since the trainship had plucked me from my childhood bunker. How many cars extended into the clouds before me? And how many behind?

"The vaccine. That's what matters. If you perfect it—in the next car—you'll keep moving up. You might run your own lab car. You might become the Conductor, one day."

"So what?"

"The recruiters told me I was going to *help* people. That's why I left my parents. All those other kids on the ground. I see now. That raider's right. We abandoned them. Just like we're abandoning this car. But that's going to change. I developed this—"

2S grabbed my arm.

"You don't want to work for Lifeline anymore? Fine. I'll take that tube. Others will."

I laughed.

"You don't understand. It's not a vaccine. Lifeline can't keep it up here. It's an anti-virus. A virus that spreads the same way as SARS-CoV20XX. Only this virus kills 20XX. If it washes away in the slush—if it goes up in the clouds—then it'll snow, it'll rain all over."

"Not going to happen. Too dangerous."

"Too late."

That pipettor had shattered flasks and flasks full of it in my labcube. I'd breathed it in. And breathed it out. 2S wrenched my fist open, grabbing for the tube, and I kicked her, slipping off the gangway as she let me go. I was falling. In the space between the clouds and the glow of Lifeline's engines, I saw: 2S shouting for help. From car after car, flurries of masked and white-coated figures emerging outside. At least one reaching for me. Yes, in that gesture, if not for me then for those on the ground, tens, hundreds, thousands of quarantines from now—I saw a cure.

Interview with Andrea Kriz

INTERSTELLAR FLIGHT PRESS: What does the future mean to you?

ANDREA KRIZ: Possibility.

IFP: How did you get your start writing?

AK: I took a short story workshop taught by Shariann Lewitt in my senior year of college. I learned about the building blocks of short fiction, as well as how to analyze my own writing critically, which really helped me improve my skills over the years. Finally, Shariann opened my mind to the worlds of science fiction and fantasy! I experimented with some of my first SFF stories in that class and haven't stopped since.

IFP: What is your favorite thing about your own writing? Or about the process of writing?

AK: The best part about writing to me is definitely 1) the beginning—daydreaming, getting the idea, first putting it into words, and 2) having a finished product I'm proud of reading and sharing. The middle part—editing, making it work—is what's difficult!

IFP: How does your identity/community/background influence your work?

AK: My parents come from diverse backgrounds, but didn't incorporate that much of their cultures into our lives when I was growing up (I don't speak either of their native languages, for example). So some of my writing comes from learning more about my heritage as an adult. Science is also a huge part of my life now, so I try to incorporate my areas of research into my writing at times.

IFP: How do you think we can build a better world as creatives?

AK: That's a tough one. I think people have always used stories as a way of showing readers a wider world and enabling them to empathize, even if not agree, with other perspectives. We need to continue doing that now, more than ever. But lately, the world seems especially hungry for speculative fiction. So I think we also have a role in imagining what the future holds—dire apocalypses, but especially creative ways in which our current problems could be solved. Importantly, unlike scientists and policymakers, we're not constrained by our current reality :)

IFP: Let us know any upcoming projects or ways our community can support you:

AK: The best way to support me is to read my work, a lot of which is available for free!

Here are a couple of other stories I've had come out lately, which I love:

Pearleater's Promise at Cossmass Infinities (2020)

Communist Computer Rap God in Clarkesworld (2021)

The Wake-Up Call

BY SUHAILA SUNDARARAJAN

Finally, someone who can help, she thinks. Finally, someone with power over them.

Tina clings to the peak of the highest mountain she can climb, like a child standing on boxes to make herself heard among elders, and focuses on crafting her message.

"They're insane. They trapped us and took us from our homes to a strange place called America. They say we don't belong there. They think they own the whole world and they're trying to wipe us off the planet. They try to kill us, and when we defend ourselves they brand *us* murderers and splash us all over their news."

"We can't take it anymore. There's a virus going around, society is crumbling, they're rioting in the streets."

A moment's hesitation. A deep breath. She completes her message:

"You've been sending us regular radio signals for years. Now would be a good time."

Minutes after Tina's call, it's 5 AM in San Francisco: two friends walking their dogs are forced to a stop by frantic barking, their dogs' eyes wide and fixed on the sky.

"Maybe a storm?" one of the friends says.

"There's not even a cloud in the sky," replies the other.

The whimpering dogs burst into a run, tugging so hard they break free, running loose through the streets. The owners run after their dogs but ultimately are left alone.

A black, pulsing shadow suddenly forms, flowing across the sky, until it completely eclipses the rising sun. Intense light bursts from the darkness. A moment later, a piercing blast and its thunderous echo roll over the Earth.

In Washington, DC, the dark cloud and thunder confuse a man as he drives to work, listening to the radio forecasting sunny weather. Google Maps doesn't do its usual job of routing through traffic. He has an early sales meeting with a prospective client in England, but after five tries, the call won't connect. The ominous sky accompanied by a bad day makes him want to cheer himself up with a cappuccino, but the ATM isn't working.

Without accurate GPS time signals, machines stop working, stock markets around the world close, and the Internet grinds to a halt.

One after another, world leaders declare states of emergency on top of COVID-19, but does anyone hear them? No one can watch satellite TV or contact long-distance family.

The President is able to contact other world leaders using emergency protected bands, but the atmosphere is full of distrust. Every leader thinks one of the others is responsible for the overloaded satellites. America's unchecked access to space has led several countries to develop anti-satellite weapons. With every ally suspect and a military rendered powerless, America is more alone than ever.

No one is shopping, jogging, driving. Across the country, everyone is standing still, staring at the dark, pulsating mass in the sky.

Feeling the warmth of the sun as the black shape loosens its form and flows freely again through the sky, Tina feels powerful, as if her body is warming up, getting ready for action. The spikes on her body absorb the light, and she naturally converts it to electrical signals that she uses to communicate with her family.

They named her Tina so she would never forget who she was: *Vespa velutina*, the Asian giant hornet. *Vespa velutina* are most active when the sun is most intense. They rely on the photovoltaic ability of their bodies to convert sunlight into electrical energy, and they emit electrical signals through small spikes all over their body to navigate and communicate with fellow hornets.

She always wondered what would happen if hornets were able to absorb more sunlight. It finally clicked when she realized that those subtle radio signals Earth had been receiving—the ones the humans had been trying to decipher unsuccessfully, that most hornets had received but ignored—those signals were sent by hornets from space. Being closer to the sun allowed them to evolve their photovoltaic abilities into a superpower compared to those of Earth hornets. *God, never let me say it's not worth trying,* Tina thinks, remembering how she took a long shot and, surprisingly, managed to make contact with the alien hornets.

Her family and friends fly to her side. The huge swarm descends from the sky and lands behind her. Humans are usually most active when the sun is bright, too, but they're so wrapped up in their own lives they don't notice anyone else. It's almost like they're sleepwalking. She watches with satisfaction as the humans buzz around hopelessly, like wasps trapped in a bottle, desperately trying to find a way out. Well, they're awake now.

Interview with Suhaila Sundararajan

INTERSTELLAR FLIGHT PRESS: What does the future mean to you?

SUHAILA SUNDARARAJAN: Some people dwell in the past, others live for the present, but I've always been a person who looks to the future. Whether it's my obsessive need to plan for next year as if it's tomorrow, or my tendency to create imaginary futures and parallel universes in my daydreams, I've always felt most at home when thinking about the future.

That said, to me the future is about opportunity and growth. The future is whatever we want it to be, based on what we do right now. If we have a picture of the future we want, it can be a map for us to follow to reach it.

IFP: How did you get your start writing?

SS: I have always been writing but this is my first time being published by anyone other than myself!

I started writing for others when I was 8 years old and started a neighborhood newsletter, which only two of my neighbors opted to read. When I was nine, my dad taught me basic HTML and set me up with a website, and I wrote articles about the Looney Toons and why Marvin the Martian was the best of them. Then I started blogging and haven't stopped since.

IFP: What is your favorite thing about your own writing? Or about the process of writing?

SS: I often start with a very vague idea of what I want to say, but once I start writing, I make connections that I didn't notice before, and what I thought I was going to say turns out very different. It feels like I'm learning from myself and it's amazing. Writing helps me process the emotions, feelings, and thoughts floating around my head.

IFP: How does your identity/community/background influence your work?

SS: I am autistic and that means my brain works differently than a neurotypical brain does. There are a few distinct styles of thinking that most autistic people gravitate toward, but my brain prefers music/math/pattern thinking. Essentially I find patterns in things, really easily. I don't think in words, but my thoughts are more like a mix between a mind map and a geometric tile mosaic... it's hard to explain. I notice patterns and parallels between things that most people don't think to connect, so I write about them.

As a Muslim, I have an interest in making a positive difference in the world and speaking out against injustice. There's a difference between telling people what to think and showing them through a story. A story can sometimes feel closer to reality than the truth.

I'm also Sri Lankan, and that combined with being Muslim and autistic makes me a person who has never read a book and seen myself in a character. I choose to write characters who are less represented and more complex, in hopes that my children and others in the coming generations will grow up finding more relatable characters.

IFP: How do you think we can build a better world as creatives?

SS: I think the best thing any creative person can do is to keep creating and create genuinely from the heart. We learn about each other through our creations, and learning about each other will lead to a better world.

IFP: Let us know any upcoming projects or ways our community can support you:

SS: I don't have any upcoming projects at the moment, but you can check out my other public writing on my Medium profile!

Beyond that, I think we should all make more of an effort to read outside of our comfort zone, and to read other voices, whether it's a book written by a person of color, or a Muslim, or an autistic person, or anyone else, with an aim to see life through someone else's perspective. Our society has so much growing to do, and it all starts with knowing each other.

Not the Knife Today

BY NATACHI MEZ

Not the knife today. Nor the gloves. Nor the rubbing alcohol. All these weeks, turned months. Hands dried and abandoned. Soaked in hand sanitizer. Isolated from my face. Floating in a room. I live alone.

My hands live alone from me. Those hands, transmitters of that virus. That sick thing that wants to make me sick thing. That sick thing ain't in me but it made me sick, and in the sleep that I can't sleep, my hands call out to me. They say, *Love me. Hold me. Let me hold you. Let me be the hands I am.*

Hands got a mouth now. Hands need to be fed. Hands starving, me too. Hands hollering. I holler back. The doorbell rings.

I answer, and there is no one there. Good. My groceries on my doormat. My hands still yelling. Me bringing the groceries into the kitchen. Me not washing those hands. Hands touching the avocados. Hands say *they're ripe.* Hands say *not the knife today* and claw at the fruit with teeth-like fingers. They clench at the fruit.

Avocado flesh lives in the creases of the palms. Hands spit out the pit. Hands feel alive. Hands dare touch my face. Hands dare feed me. I am fed. I am hollering. I am not clean. I am not awake.

Those hands tap me gently in the morning. Say *look, the sky isn't crying today. Who knows how long we'll be cloudless.* Hands turn on the light.

Splash water in my face. Hands put on my mask for me, secure the elastic loops over my ears. Hands take me on a walk. Hands cover my eyes from the man that looks like he want to claw the fruit of my body out with his teeth-like fingers. Hands reach for the tools I keep in my pocket. I say *not the knife today.*

So hands show me a map of their palms instead. Tell me that the creases are not coincidental. Tell me the creases track each moment, and path crossed, bridge trekked, and mountain climbed, to get to you.

I say, *to me?*

Hands say, *where you wanna go?* I touch the map, and we transport, to where we are. I am with my hands. Those hands be my hands. Birthed from many hands. Reflecting hands I've never touched but have touched me.

I don't live alone. I am not alone.

Interview with Natachi Mez

INTERSTELLAR FLIGHT PRESS: What does the future mean to you?

NATACHI MEZ: The future is something deeply connected to the present, to the past. The future for me represents lineage as well as possibility. The future is a dreamspace, and also the canvas of what precedes it, made of the same stuff that precedes it. The future cannot be touched directly, and so is shaped by what occurs in the now.

IFP: How did you get your start writing?

NM: Writing has been a way for me to process my experiences and converse with myself since I was young. My first memory of keeping a journal was in kindergarten —spiral notebooks filled with playground adventures and elementary school crushes. It was a space for me to ask, ponder, and express without judgment. Writing also became a space where I responded to what I was reading. I remember making songs for characters in books.

IFP: What is your favorite thing about your own writing? Or about the process of writing?

NM: For me, writing feels both introspective and generative, an entryway into myself and how I connect with the world around me. There are times when I feel that nothing of value can run from my pen, but the act of showing up and giving time to the process of writing continues to teach me new things and be a form of adventure. I am consistently in awe of that adventure, of not knowing what or how things may come out of my writing, while also have the agency to work through and mold that writing. My favorite thing about my own writing is the rhythmic and lyrical quality — writing that makes me utter the words aloud, writing that feels like a full-body experience.

IFP: How does your identity/community/background influence your work?

NM: I am a first-generation Nigerian American woman who grew up in a Christian household. I often think about what I've inherited from my identities and the genealogies of that inheritance. Additionally, I often consider the global impacts of displacement and colonialism. While there are many wounds in these relationships, I also consider the nourishment and strength that persists. Additionally, I experiment with the concept of secular holiness, examining what worship and ritual can mean beyond a religious context.

IFP: How do you think we can build a better world as creatives?

NM: By having listening be a part of the creative process. Listening and recognizing and honoring the forces, relationships, and environments that enable us to be. By being intimate with the world, in our local corners, and beyond, sensing what nourishes and what depletes, and attempting to nourish. By knowing not one person has to do it all, that not one person can do it all. By working in concert with other beings, and by recognizing smalls can sum to something greater.

IFP: Let us know any upcoming projects or ways our community can support you:

NM: You can keep up with my latest projects and joyful expressions on Instagram, follow my weekly newsletter Soul Food Sundays for weekly doses of nourishment to your inbox, and stream my recent song P.O.A on major streaming platforms.

A Timely Mistake

BY ARCHITA MITTRA

After the murder, her device refused to glow. She turned the body over, wondering if the knife wound wasn't deep enough, and saw that it was a different face.

Aer, the Looper, had killed the wrong man.

Some accidents aren't supposed to happen, she thought, running down the stairs. It was why they sent people like her, to keep the causal loops intact. *Did the scientists from the Academy make a mistake? Did she read the map wrong?*

She had no way of knowing, just as she had no way of going home.

A few blocks away, she careened into an all-night diner, out of breath. She needed a place to sit down and figure something out. The device, designed to resemble a smartphone of this era, lay in her lap, inert. She cradled her head in her hands, fighting back tears.

Without the device, she had no way of contacting the Academy or sending a message to Zel. Zel, who was to meet her at an immersive gaming arcade, two hundred and eighteen years into the future. They'd bond over their love for games and a week after, Zel would ask her to be her "co-pilot".

It would take Aer a solid minute to realize Zel was asking her out.

"Would you like some coffee?" asked the waitress, interrupting her reverie. The woman wore a mask and had bright red hair. *Just like Zel*, Aer realized. Back in Arcadia, one could customize their body however they wished once they came of age. She'd chosen black curls, dusky skin, and a lithe nimble frame, inspired by a game character.

"Yes," said the Looper. "Why are you wearing a mask?"

The waitress frowned. "Don't you know, there's a new virus in town?"

Aer returned to the empty apartment and locked herself in, going through the facts again and again, even as the plague raged. *The Academy made a mistake and the wrong person died*, she thought, while tinkering with her device, willing it to send a signal.

It was supposed to be a quick one-day mission. The scientists had shown her pictures from the archives, the murder of a certain politician that set into motion a chain of events that led to the future. She had practiced that moment countless times in the simulations. She couldn't have messed this up.

The murder caused quite an uproar, but the police never came knocking and instead blamed it on a conspiracy by one of his rivals.

Guilt squirmed within her.

Creating Arcadia hadn't been easy, a fact that was drilled into the students of the Academy from the first day. The perfect future existed because its past already did and to maintain the state of equilibrium — continuum, they explained, was essentially a series of interlocking Bootstrap paradoxes — they had to keep sending Loopers back, so that the events happened the way they did to always lead to Arcadia.

Perhaps another Looper, lost in space and time, had made a mistake. She could try tracking down her original target, but she didn't even know where to look; besides, taking actions unsanctioned by the Academy was prohibited. What if she made things worse?

The best time travelers are the ones who don't question anything. They simply do as they're told, Zel had stated once.

She wondered now if it had been an insult. After all, she'd aced the training program.

The diner shut down after a week, as did most places. The streets were mostly empty, and a radio she'd stolen while hunting for rations, announced the ever-rising death toll in a detached voice. As countries scrambled in a race to stock up on masks and ventilators, she felt weirdly ashamed, as a being from the future, she was immune to most diseases of the past.

There'd been countless plagues and eventually humanity always found a cure. There were a few which required a nudge from the future, but this wasn't one of them or she'd have remembered.

But Aer didn't have much to do, and that *itched*. The video games felt like cave-paintings, compared to the immersive experiences she was familiar with. Nano-bots weren't invented yet, which made the process of developing a vaccine incredibly slow.

Perhaps she was in a wrong timeline, but she knew that was impossible. The mathematicians at the Academy studied the Butterfly Effect and did the complex arithmetic of plotting timelines and then, based on that data, the engineers designed the simulations.

She considered finding a different politician to kill, but decided against it, as it seemed too callous. She couldn't gamble away the future and risk erasing Zel from existence.

But what if you already did?

Every night, she cradled the silent device to her bosom, tears trailing down her cheeks. *Zel, I miss you so much.*

She'd kissed Zel for the first time, right after she'd returned from her first mission (guide a writer to publish a seminal book on quantum theory), blushing from her success. Everything she did, all the sacrifices the other travelers made, were for love, to keep the people that made up Arcadia, alive.

Aer needed more information. She snuck into a library, looking up records of this present, to find a sign or the right event to influence. In her loneliness, she sat about tracing Zel's family tree, wracking her brains to remember what little Zel had said about her ancestors and trying to connect the dots with some educated guesswork.

Casual loops couldn't have mistakes.

Yet it seemed as though the coordinates to her home never existed, as though Arcadia had vanished into thin air.

But if my past is destroyed, how am I still here?

A month later she was back at the diner. It was still closed but she had to meet someone. If her research was right, this was her only tie to Zel, the only way she could leave behind a message. Trembling with trepidation, she knocked on the door and the masked waitress appeared.

"Can I please speak to the owner?" she asked.

"My husband's been hospitalized. The doctors don't know if he will make it," the waitress replied.

If... no... Zel would never be born.

Fuck the Academy, with its rules.

"What's the way to the hospital?"

They didn't believe her when she said she was immune, so she barged into one of the wards and kissed a patient. That convinced one of the doctors to take her blood sample and test it.

If the vaccine worked, she'd have a new set of problems. She'd never meet Zel again, but perhaps Zel would still live in a world without her, a world that was not Arcadia. And Aer would be stuck here, alone and disguised, with a different name and a new life.

Saddened, she looked out of the window, into the silent and empty city, and then the device in her pocket slowly started to glow.

Interview with Archita Mittra

INTERSTELLAR FLIGHT PRESS: What does the future mean to you?

ARCHITA MITTRA: Hope, I suppose, though at this point I'd just go with "uncertain". As a child, I'd imagine the future as this wonderful place-where I'm happy and my problems have faded and everyone is nice and kind. A place where I'm more confident, with a greater sense of purpose and the world is more just and inclusive. I guess we're still working towards it. But with the covid crisis turning everything topsy-turvy, I'm not so sure anymore. It feels more apocalyptic than Utopian. So now, it's like an uncharted territory that I'm curious about but not too eager to explore.

IFP: How did you get your start writing?

AM: I've been writing and making art for as long as I remember, though art was always my first love. I've always kept diaries and lists and filled the backs of my notebooks with poems. In high school, I started working for The Statesman- writing articles and covering local events- for the children's supplement "Voices" that came out every Thursday. Around the same time, I realized how much I enjoyed English literature as a subject, prompting me to later major in it. Of course, I'm immensely grateful to my parents, who always encouraged me to create, read books, watch movies, and generally do my own thing, without ever pressurizing me to study or finish my homework.

Initially, I was more of a "poetry" person, though, for the last two-three years, I've gravitated more towards short fiction.

IFP: What is your favorite thing about your own writing? Or about the process of writing?

AM: I think I've always approached writing as a sort of jigsaw puzzle. As a writer, I have all the pieces that I have to fit them as exactly as I can, though usually it doesn't happen and that's frustrating. But the sheer joy that comes from when a piece or two fits- the plot strands come together, I've found the right word, the characters feel utterly real- that's very satisfying. I really love the brainstorming and ideating, and the times when the writing seems effortless and just "flows". Editing my own work, on the other hand, scares the living daylights out of me and I feel like I'm fumbling in a locked room for treasure, with all the lights out.

IFP: How does your identity/community/background influence your work?

AM: I'm a 23-year-old writer, based in Kolkata, India. My pronouns are she/her and I identify as queer (biromantic and somewhere on the asexual spectrum) although my schooling and the homophobic culture most of us grew up in, denied me access to this "western" vocabulary and I've spent a lot of time questioning myself, without ever being sure of my answers. My mother tongue is Bengali, which is the language I speak with my family, although I grapple with the guilt of not reading/writing much in that medium, preferring English instead. I've faced a fair share of colourism, misogyny, abuse, and racism- being bullied for my "stutter", for my "dark skin", for being "weird" and so on, and I suppose all of it, unconsciously feeds its way back to my writing.

Most of my stories have female protagonists, battling identity issues and trauma, and are sad or lonely or both. I think the problem with grief and the way we often represent it, is that we often see it through a lens of a "loss of power" and we strive for ways to give back that power, agency, closure, whatever. And that's certainly important, but as with the case of so many mental illnesses and societal inequalities, not everything has a "perfect solution", not everything can be cured or solved, and even if it could, it probably isn't accessible to everyone. And that, in turn, makes me want to write stories about sad girls specifically more- girls who feel alone and alienated and powerless and think that the world is too much for them, and that's absolutely not their fault but of the world, they were born into. Injustice may make a lot of us angry and itch for revolution, but it can also make some of us really sad and affect us in insidious ways. Assertive strong-willed female heroines like Wonder Woman can make for great role models, but not everyone has the mental strength, resources, or even the privilege to be like that (which isn't to say female superheroes are not important- they are and we need more of them!) and that being vulnerable, emotional and "soft" aren't necessarily negative, even if the world treats them as weaknesses. You don't have to save the world. You may not even be able to save yourself. But you must try, and it's okay to just be able to make it, just able to survive- being able to live through each day is still a victory.

IFP: How do you think we can build a better world as creatives?

AM: As creatives, our greatest resource is our ability to imagine and empathize- we can use our art to connect to other people, come up with ingenious solutions, and tell the stories that the world needs. While we need to accept and acknowledge our limitations, we still have the power to change existing narratives and imagine a world that is diverse, inclusive, and kind. Stories get into people's heads, and we need to tell the stories that aren't being told or are being forcibly silenced for whatever reason.

IFP: Let us know any upcoming projects or ways our community can support you:

AM: Most of my creative projects are a work-in-progress and I like dabbling through several hobbies at once, be it calligraphy, baking, or discovering a new card game. I'm always open to freelance writing, editing, teaching, and other creative projects and I occasionally review books of poetry or of the fantasy/sci-fi-/speculative variety. Under the name "Fableheart", I run an art+crafts page and make and sell jewelry on Instagram. I also offer tarot and runic readings for anyone who is interested. I'm presently working on editing some of my short stories, refining the rules of a few games I've come up with, and revamping my blog. You can say hello to me on Twitter, Instagram.

Unwilled

BY NISOLA JEGEDE

Alungba, queen of the African continent, sat on a floating, iron basket, barely moving except for clenching and unclenching her jaws. Her wide, usually flabby ears were taut as she listened to the cries and moans surging from the shimmering Orb of Confusion, held mid-air by her third and fourth eyes. She was the eighth god in the golden hut, alongside six members of the Rood—leaders of the other continents—and Eledua, Lord of the Rood. A humming robot repaired the thick, gold-encrusted walls of the hut.

The air was pregnant with anger and frustration. The events of the earth were presented by the Orb of Confusion: its interior clouded with streams and puffs of smoke, and its exterior hung with a mixture of furiously dancing fire and thunder, the pain the people of the earth were experiencing. These feelings agitated Alungba's mind, clouded her head alongside the humans' shrills. Her long nails held on tightly to her chair. She had the power to remove the gory sights that filled the Orb, she and the other gods, but none of them did that.

Murfu, the tallest among the leaders, bounced his third leg aggressively on the breathing, moving floor creating dents in it and the ground howled. Eere went on his knee and pinched the breathing ground. The ground howled again and Murfu laughed. At the corner of the hut Makana was balling and unballing herself, and Eledua sat above the celestial sphere of the hut with his eyes of fire closed while his face rested on his rocky hands.

Alungba looked up at the center of the hut where Eledua was and her gaze turned scornful. She knew he watched the events in the orb through his skin despite not being seated among the members of the Rood but would only react if there was chaos between the gods in the golden hut. How dare they? How dare the gods' offspring punish her offspring for something as trivial as skin color? How dare they make her offspring susceptible to all manners of ill words and punishments when she, Alungba, the mother of nature, had done everything to keep the earth on balance? Though they hurt, she refused to unglue her first and second eyes from the Orb. Alungba wished something could be done, as she concentrated on the images engorged in chaos.

Not that the humans' groans would change anything, not that all the gods would be able to come together to nudge their offspring to love one another. When she told the members of the Rood, with fury and disdain, to warn their offspring off her children what did they do in reply? They laughed.

They laughed at her, Alungba!

Murfu's single-arm hit Alungba's basket chair as he stamped the floor, Alungba stared at his retreating back with contempt. She bared her tiny, surplus teeth to stop any words from flowing from her mouth. Then Alungba laughed hard. The harder she laughed, her stomach expanded releasing the fresh fragrance of greens, oceans, and mountains. The smell of Africa. Just like the ruler and king of Africa that she was, Alungba's dark skin glowed and her body expanded. Moisture covered her being before it flowed to the moving ground, within moments, seedlings took its place. The other members of the Rood would know what it meant to deal with Africa, her child continent.

Alungba called the king of Blights, its faceless, grim presence filled her with a sense of satisfaction for the first time.

"Go and disturb the earth with a plague they have never encountered," she ordered.

The King of Blights lowered its stiffly hanging tail that was poised behind him and stamped its pronged feet.

"H-h-how much can I torment them?" it asked, its chirpy voice dripping with glee.

"As much as much as you want."

Its jaws dropped, showing its toothlessness before it disappeared quickly as if scared she would retract her order.

The other members of the Rood laughed harder.

"My offspring are smart, they will find the cure immediately," Eere said, stressing the word, immediately.

Alungba looked at the other members of the Rood and felt their glee towards the agony of her offspring. The agony caused by their offspring.

"They always find cures because I control the King of Blights and give them the power to do so. They won't have that this time." The atmosphere in the hut went still and Alungba felt their fear. She smiled.

"Until everyone is ready to bring peace among our offspring, the plague remains." Their eyes instantly went to the orb in the hut.

What she did not tell the other members of the Rood was that there was a cure buried in an unexpected place in Africa. This brought about a change in the track of Alungba's anger. This time, her contempt was on her offspring. How come none of them made any attempt to get the cure that had been planted under their noses? How could they forget, for a moment, that they were made to be kings? Had they forgotten the lengths she went to for them to be crowned on the thrones of the Land of Goodwill? How dare they forget the Great Fight, the war she fought with the members of the Rood to secure the Land of Goodwill for them alone! Yes, her people still maintained their fighting spirits, but towards what? Serving others? Who taught them servitude? The voices in Alungba's head screamed these questions at her.

Alungba winced as she pulled a strong strand of her fully blown afro to calm those voices. The voices quieted, but pushed blood towards her third and fourth eyes, making them release their hold on the orb. Darkness filled the thatched hut.

Interview with Nisola Jegede

INTERSTELLAR FLIGHT PRESS: What does the future mean to you?

NISOLA JEGEDE: The future refers to the period of unity and peace between nations, races, and genders. It is a time in which the precocious science and technology would be considered for the positive evolution of the world. The future is a period that people would not be afraid of becoming their real selves.

IFP: How did you get your start writing?

NJ: I started about eight years ago. Due to the ghetto-ish surroundings in which I was raised, I lived through several unusual events. Also, my childhood is spiced by several mythological stories I heard, alongside my friends and sisters, from my maternal grandmother at night. Hence, when I began to write, my stories were a mixture of the events I encountered while growing up and the tales my grandmother told me. I started writing to entertain my friends and to keep the records of some situations. "Unwilled" will be my first published story.

IFP: What is your favorite thing about your own writing? Or about the process of writing?

NJ: The favorite thing about my writing is that it is rooted in Africanfuturism. That is, futurism rooted in the African society. In most part of the world, African traditions, cultures, and technologies have been deemed backward or unworthy. I like the fact that I am writing about the African culture in relation to the machine age.

However, when it comes to the process of writing stories, I enjoy the fact that I simply reimagine the ways and methods of African gods and goddesses and represent them through characters. It makes writing seems like lesser work.

IFP: How does your identity/community/background influence your work?

NJ: I learned from my grandmother that her lineage worshipped *Yeye Osun* before the foreign religions swamped Nigeria. *Yeye Osun,* the Yoruba goddess who is associated with water, is like the Greek's Hera in a way. She represents motherhood, fertility, love, and purity. Her worshippers often wear white. I love the stories about her a lot. In the university, when my class was given an assignment to portray our cultures, I represented her. She is one of the strongest goddesses in the Yoruba Pantheon. I create my protagonists based on her deeds and works.

IFP: How do you think we can build a better world as creatives?

NJ: I believe writers and other creatives can build a better world by focusing on creating an optimistic future. That is, they should focus on encouraging the people in the world to see themselves as one. They should create stories that would make people understand that most times, we have one common enemy. This enemy might appear in different ways. Truth be told, the past of several societies have been filled with blood and discord. Wars and disagreements may have ended but their residuals are still present in too many hearts. However, if we are to dwell on the past, the world might not attain the much-desired unity.

IFP: Let us know any upcoming projects or ways our community can support you:

NJ: I have embarked on another writing project. It is a story of a female that is sent to the world to deliver people from the clutches of greed and unfairness. It would be a thing of joy if the community would read my story.

That way, the hard work and determination that birth the story would worth it.

Saving Grace

BY JUSTIN C. KEY

January 8th, 4120

The fact that Jayde Hairston, sole commander of the GSC *Regret*, was awake meant that humanity had succumbed to the virus thousands of years ago. If her service was no longer needed, the Ghana Space Centre would have signaled *Regret* to reverse course or terminate life support. Instead, Jayde sat in the cramped spacecraft, stiff and dry from suspension, reviewing her neural files before crossing Behemoth's event horizon. She knew her mission: sacrifice her material self to the black hole and change the past.

Red light flashed in her periphery. She pinched her ear to initiate a download of humanity's last letters to her, then stopped. She hadn't earned them yet.

Regret began to rattle. Its many-windowed walls turned malleable.

Unannounced tears dislodged and fell vertically towards the ship's backend. They elongated into thin translucencies. Jayde herself began to stretch . . .

Jayde opened what she thought were eyes; a hundred windows opened with them. Too many. A past Earth waited beyond each. She closed these 'eyes', concentrated, and recalled her briefing. Behemoth's gravitational pull had destroyed both ship and body. Only consciousness and time persisted. Everything else was a derivative construct of the two. *Regret*—with its windows and control panels—had been designed to give her consciousness structure.

She pictured her heart pumping life through intricate highways and imagined organs and tissue and skin filling the body in around it. She willed her 'heart' to slow and felt the calm. Thought begat sensation. She had toes when she thought to move them, an itch when she thought to scratch. She'd become a mercurial canvas, a lifetime's worth of memory, emotion tactility painting her reality.

She tried sight again. *Regret* was back to limited size and windows. She moved towards one. Blue curves with white swirls cradled a textured, colorful land. The United States of America. Analysis of the sun, moon, and background stars gave the date: January 16th, 2020. Right on time.

Light, spilling from somewhere. Jade decided it came from an adjacent window, an adjacent time. She turned —

No distractions! Stay the course. Prevent covid-US.

That was her mission. Just observing any other window—any other timeline —could have quantum implications.

She flipped the lever to start transmission to the US of A, felt air fill her lungs, and . . .

. . . turned to look. Elsewhere.

The other window overlooked her home continent, from which all human life had sprung. She didn't need algorithms to know she was observing world-lines from the beginning of the Atlantic Slave Trade. Ghana's physicists postulated that only electromagnetic waves could be sent back in time. Perfect for modern computer systems, but what else was possible? Could she change the course of history as the booming voice of God?

Jayde's mother had been intentional in telling her their family's lineage. How they were snatched from the Great Continent to help build the country that would bring humanity to the brink of extinction. Then the black flight to African nations to escape an empire collapsing under the weight of a mutated virus sitting on a foundation weak with oppression.

Jayde imagined slave ships tracing the Atlantic. China birthed COVID-19, America matured it, but this is where the real pandemic began.

Crackles from the 2020 United States window. "This is a secure line. Identify yourself."

"I'm Jayde," she said, still looking down at her home. Thoughts of her childhood, the freedom of play, the wonders of the University. Jayde had not learned to fear coronavirus until adulthood, young and in love with her budding family. A medical missionary had brought back the devastating mutated pathogen from quarantined America. It spread quickly and without mercy. Jayde's world crumbled as she became a family of one. Space offered both refuge and redemption.

"Okay, Jayde? I think you have the wrong frequency."

Jayde clenched her eyes. They almost felt real. "This is Captain Hairston of Airship *Regret*. I represent the Ghanaian Union."

"That's great. Good luck with that."

"You are Professor Aaron Durham, date of birth oh-two, zero-six, nineteen-sixty-eight, director of SETI's Defense Against Time sector. I am invoking Code Tempus Fugit three-four-jay-six-eighty-nine-twenty."

Tense silence followed. Archaeologists had scoured America's records for a possible cure, instead finding a treasure trove of code phrases and their implications. *Tempus Fugit* was for time travel.

"I'll put you through to the president."

"Please don't," she said.

"Thank god. What is this about?"

Her consciousness oscillated in uncertainty. She was a descendant of free people, still doing work for those who had sought to chain them so long ago.

"I'll show you," she said. "Are you on a computer?"

"I am."

She touched her ear. A symbolic gesture in her incorporeal form, but she knew no other way to transmit. Faintly, she heard the edge of 45's voice. The transmission was successful; the neural downloads had survived Jayde's transition. The greatest quantum physicists, historians, and computer programmers had forged the Presidential Address to give the United States the best chance to reverse its disastrous course without destroying the space-time continuum. At least, that's what they had told her.

"This deep fake is the best I've seen," the man on the other end said. Then, somberly, "The president will never approve."

"Put it in today's briefing. His pride won't let him admit he didn't read it. Air the video right before his rally tomorrow. Then tell him everything. Emphasize that campaigning on leading the world fight against covid means re-election. He'll gladly take credit for the whole thing. Included is a full follow-up speech for his rally."

"I'm reading it. Sounds just like him." Then, "Is that true? He'll win re-election?"

"We don't know. Without intervention, there won't be another election. Godspeed."

"Wait, how—"

She cut the feed, as planned. She'd said enough.

The deed done, she glanced over at other world-lines. Had she made the right decision? Should she have confronted that initial travesty? Perhaps risking the dismantling of space and time was worth America never becoming such an existential threat.

Jayde closed her eyes. She couldn't think of that now. The past was the past. At this irony, she laughed vibrations through the cosmos. The red light gently reminded her of waiting messages. She touched her ear, let them flow, and delighted in their hope. Only once did it occur to her that success meant she would never be born. If this was nonexistence then, she welcomed it.

Interview with Justin C. Key

INTERSTELLAR FLIGHT PRESS: What does the future mean to you?

JUSTIN C. KEY: Different things. I am a father of three, my youngest only a few months old. So the future means their future, their rights, their quality of life, their wonders and their freedom to wonder. As a life-long learner, the future means continuing to discover ourselves, our world, and our place in the universe. The future means hope for equality but also acknowledging that more opportunity can breed more disparities depending on a society's ever-changing power dynamics. I have hope for the future because I can't help but to hope for myself and for my children. But I also have fear, because I know our history.

IFP: How did you get your start writing?

JK: Like many, I was an avid reader as a child and devoured all kinds of books. From *Goosebumps* and *Animorphs* to Richard Wright's *Black Boy* and Stephen King's *IT,* I covered the whole spectrum. I soon found myself wanting to create. I wrote, illustrated, and bound a short book called *The Butterfly Chronicles* in fourth grade (man, I wish I could find it) and in high school wrote fanfic for my favorite video game, *Halo* (that, I do have and it will never see the light of day if I have any say over it).

When I was 20 and halfway through college I sat down to write my first novel. Luckily, that summer I also read Stephen King's *On Writing* and internalized his 'first one million words are practice' rule. I continued to write, chipping away at my million, and found joy in the process. I've written several novels, each with their own lessons, and have more recently focused on short stories to hone my craft, explore a lot of my ideas in a shorter time line, and rediscover that thrill that at times gets lost in the long and arduous process of revising a novel.

IFP: What is your favorite thing about your own writing? Or about the process of writing?

JK: I've found dialogue to be the most enjoyable part of writing. Getting it right can be difficult, but it can really bring a character to life and make their voice fun to discover on the page. As for process, I enjoy the discovery in that first draft (I'm mostly a 'pantser') and the satisfaction of turning a block of vomit-words into (what I hope is) beautiful prose. With this piece, for example, I enjoyed navigating all the big themes I was going for and trimming it down to a flash piece. What's essential? What am I really trying to say? How can I use my experience with the English language to make this 13-word sentence into a 9-word sentence that says the same thing and, as a bonus, even more?

IFP: How does your identity/community/background influence your work?

JK: I am an African-American cis-gender, straight male who grew up in Southeast DC in the 90s. A lot of things have shaped my identity, from going to all-black schools, being raised by a single mother, losing family members to gun violence, and seeing the various life paths taken by my peers. Another important thing that has shaped my work as a writer is that I grew up reading mostly stories about people who didn't look like me. This is important because when I sat down to write that first novel in college, my protagonist was blond-haired and blue-eyed. Because the books that I read with black characters usually made their blackness a main trait, I had this automatic thought that to have a black character meant I had to say something about them being black, when in the beginning I just wanted to tell stories. As I've grown (personally, professionally, and as a parent) I've broadened my reading library and have become more adept at telling a version of my own story instead of the default story. I want black and brown characters to be as common as their white counterparts and without need for explanation, justification, or apologies.

As a psychiatrist and a medical doctor, my writing has naturally evolved to reflect my experiences, knowledge, and want for change. There has been an increased sense of responsibility as I use my relatively unique life perspective to inform my stories and create characters and narratives that not only entertain, but evoke self-reflection and, in some cases, change.

IFP: How do you think we can build a better world as creatives?

JK: By having a sense of responsibility and care towards those we aim to represent in our writing. By remembering that some of our audience may have limited exposure to diverse backgrounds, and our representations of them in our stories can subconsciously (or consciously) contribute to or combat assumptions.

That and imagining bright futures to inspire hope in the otherwise hopeless and dark endings to warn against the potential failings of a complacent society.

IFP: Let us know any upcoming projects or ways our community can support you:

JK: Please consider my other recent and upcoming work:

"One Hand in The Coffin" *Strange Horizons* (2020) and *Nightlight Podcast* (2020).

"The Perfection of Theresa Watkins" out now from *Tor.com* (2020).

Upcoming stories in Escape Pod, Don't Touch That parenting anthology, The Magazine of Fantasy & Science Fiction, and Cadwell Turnbull's MANY-WORLD's collaborative project.

You can follow my journey at my website, Twitter, and Instagram.

Season of Safety

BY TLOTLO TSAMAASE

CW: This story contains descriptions of domestic violence. If you or someone you know is experiencing domestic violence during the pandemic, call 1–800–799-SAFE to find resources in your area.

Wednesday, April 1

Through our front window, smoke tangles with falling winter leaves, sweeps through the fronds of tree branches; a birdsong breeze washes out the silent cries of a woman in a tiny low-income home. It is the norm, and nearby surveillant eyes will breathe no truth, will snitch not, for every breath's soul is tied down, a creature refusing to escape its restraints. Inside, the woman is me, folded on the floor like adjustable furniture, knees nutty beneath the skin, but healable, the legs still functional to scurry about to serve him.

The withering smoke squeezes itself through the slithering crack in our window. Into our home. Into us. It was only that one time he'd hit me in front of our kids; my hands could barely silence my screams, I'd never meant for them to see. A lush of daylight struggles through the two grime-clad windows. Spotty fingerprints on the window from the time my babies' fears screamed for life.

Last night, when he found out that we'll be going into lockdown, he stained my amygdala with a fistful of passion. This morning, the post-coital pain rides my backbone as my five-year-old helps me get up with her tiny, chubby hands. Nowadays, I can't tell the difference between sex and violence; he is passionate as he is violent. What does that make me if I enjoy it sometimes?

Violence tastes like a summer song in our wintry days. I miss the long drives we used to take to my parents' farm, the summer sun beating down on the tarmac, and songs warm and soft adding more love into the tide of our breaths. Our good memories were always filled with summer songs, until he flipped, slapped me for the first time and now each violent act tastes like a summer song.

Our home is not divided into rooms such as an enclosed kitchen, a bedroom, nor a bathroom. Ours is only one room, the bathing area in the corner is separated by a flimsy bedsheet, hung from the ceiling with a rope that he tied around my neck once for the unprepared meal and his after-work hunger. We're five—me, my boyfriend, and three children: 2, 5, and 7. There is nowhere to hide from him. The house is 6mx3m, essentially 18m2 of torture.

Thursday, April 2

Adjacent to the house is the outdoor cooking area, barricaded with loose concrete blocks to shield from the wind, tarpaulin as a makeshift roof held up by the stem of wood.

The burning cold of winter clings to our soles as we sit around the outdoor fire, inhaling smoke and stories and lies. I wasn't meant to be here, but this is where my decisions led me. I fell in love and thought that love was safe, but sometimes what we think is safe is suicide. I kiss my daughter's tiny fingers as she drinks her milk, my other two eating their dinner quietly.

I stare out of our yard, past the wiry boundary fence, and look at every home so identical to ours, walls dirt-stained, corrugated roofs falling apart, every life so poor like us unable to free itself. We live a stone's throw away from the rich; if you cross the road and walk briskly past the neighborhood supermarket, you'll find a private school, houses of wealth, and space blithely buffered from our poverty by high boundary walls and landscaped lawns. I bet you their lockdown isn't as horrendous as ours.

Poverty birthed me and kept close to my parents like a mollycoddling grandmother so they tossed me into varsity wishing my education will emancipate them. Their wishes wilted on the sill of our hope, when in second year it was tough living on the meager government allowance we received as students, so I met men. Blessers, really. Everything I could ever dream of was funded. I look back at the sizable money that could have afforded me a house near the city, which I instead used all on clothes, weaves, perfumes, alcohol-fueled nights with other guys I was romantically linked to, so my blesser, in a jealous spat, would withhold money from me until I resumed my loyalty to him.

My parents stay up north 8–10 hours from us, are elderly, and don't need their desperate daughter to potentially infect them. When you have no luck like a wealthy relative, or anyone who can offer a place, the only thing you can do is stay in hell, a hell lesser than the hell out there.

Saturday, April 4

He comes home today in fists and anger. "The bastards fired me." He punches the wall; his anger ripples, burns the air to a crisp. My children stay in one corner quivering as I try to soothe him. "What the fuck are we supposed to do now?" He pushes me aside and punches and kicks his anger out into me. Then he sits on the stoop, simmering. "Look what you made me do now," he says. "We won't have income, and you all sit there eating everything as if money falls from the sky."

There's a ban for the sale of alcohol in the country, and his withdrawal symptoms are pissing him off. Honestly, I thought that if he's off alcohol it'd be easier. But, no. All he thinks about is the potential income lost, and all this time at home. When I call for help, I'm asked who the house belongs to. To him. Nothing can be done. He finds me under a tree "betraying" him "after everything I have done for you," he shouts and beats me with the nearest branch.

Sunday, April 5

I've no phone—my boyfriend sleeps with it tied to his neck. He still thinks I'm trying to betray him. I can't even call the police.

I've no money; he forces me by the throat and demands I give him the house money passwords, with that he transfers all the money into his account.

"This is the only way we can perfectly manage our finances," he says. Then he confiscates my bank card, memorizes the pin.

I can't talk to the neighbors; they're under the thumb of their husbands. If word gets out to my boyfriend, I could be dead, I think; but no, he wouldn't go that far.

Isolation is his ally: I have no contact with anyone.

Tuesday, April 7

My boyfriend worked at a supermarket that paid him P900 monthly, whilst his CEO received a monthly retainer of P1,000,000. He seethes about this daily. "P1 million yet the fucker can't increase our salary by just P2,000, nje." He storms up and down the house. "This is what we're going to do: put a table out there and sell anything."

"We're not allowed to do that," I say, crouched by the door.

He raises his hand and I flinch. "Stop coming up with problems and bring solutions to the table." He chews on his thumb's nail. "They're only helping formal businesses. What about us?"

I stare at my own son, a reproduction of my boyfriend who I met in second year of Business Studies as a blesser. After a couple of months of dating him, he said he wanted a kid, and I gave it to him because he loved me and I loved him, and I regret letting my parents and him convince me to drop out from varsity and stay home. He promised them that he'd marry me that he'd send his uncles over for lobola discussions. Then he started ignoring their calls. Suddenly it was years later, three children later and I had to get a job, with no degree, which was only cleaning houses and banks.

Before, I complied with his beatings because he paid for my well-being when government varsity allowance couldn't cover certain amenities. He was a big contractor back in the day, winning tenders and running a successful electrical engineering company, which funded the expensive cars, the big homes, the first-class travels—and if it weren't enough, loans filled the gaps. His company fell through—and he lost everything. Now he ruins everything he touches, even us.

Is there a better future after this? I don't know. I can't leave home for now, for my children, for me. How many of the souls in our breaths have people like him taken from women like me? No, this can't go on any longer, for I fear that my boyfriend is going to turn into my murderer.

Thursday, April 9

He is frustrated this morning. Refused me my phone and used all my airtime to talk to a friend about a potential deal. Said it's my fault the deal didn't go through because my airtime finished. We've all lost control of our lives and our businesses and the only control he has is his grip around my throat. "Look, what you made me do. If only you'd listened."

Saturday, April 11

This morning, my employer from the bank inboxed me. My boyfriend didn't let me look at the message. Without looking at me, he said, "Unless you want to leave me alone with the kids, tell them that you have a right to not come in to work given the circumstances." He didn't have to strangle me or beat me to sway me. It would be like entrusting your children to a pedophile.

Why did I stay? How did I stay this long? Why would I let it get this far? I just never thought it'd get this bad, a heartless-kind-of-bad of literally hurting your own child. You're the frog in the pot, the water infinitesimally reaching the boiling point, but you don't realize you're burning until you're dead. If our relationship had started out starkly this way, I'd have run. Run and never tied myself down with his kids. *My* kids—I love them to death.

I know how crazy that sounds, but back then high on adrenaline, shit was muddled up in my mind. During my varsity years, I'd get bouts of depression, and regardless of how late into the night it was or how hectic his work life was, he'd always drive to the dorms and hold me as I cried into his arms. That was the first man who didn't use me for sex or call me emotional. He love-bombed me, checking in daily, and even paid for my therapy. I'd never known comfort like that, I felt safe in his arms, felt the love. And now it's all gone.

So my boyfriend sits, balancing on the stool as he rocks back and forth, casually slicing parts of an apple, chewing it, spitting out the seeds as I cleanly and confidently telephonically talk to my manager without distress explaining to them why I can't come to work. Satisfied, my boyfriend hops up, kisses my face, caresses me, confesses how he now trusts and loves me.

And smack me now, but I feel this tugging feeling in my stomach, a bit of bliss that I make him happy. My hormones are haywire, I'm losing my mind.

Tuesday, April 14

A friend of mine living in Ginger ran out onto the streets the other day, just ran and ran until police stopped her and fined her P5,000, which is six times her salary. Even though she fled a burning abusive home, they fined her, didn't want to hear her grievances, was told to go straight home and follow procedure. When she returned home, her husband beat her for the fine until there was no more breath in her. Her only son witnessed everything. If there was a safety measure for our dire circumstance, she'd still be alive.

Sunday, April 19

He applied for an essential permit through the government website to conduct delivery of "incomprehensible words" and was rejected today. I don't know what delivery he wanted to do, but he's angry that the government is "a motherfucking asshole that only helps foreigners." I agree and tell him he is smart. He is quick with a back-handed slap, and it knocks me down. Says I must watch my sarcastic mouth.

I must get a permit to go to the store, I could take advantage of that outing to obtain a reprieve from him. I have no airtime to go online or call anyone. "If you don't stop over-eating I'm putting you out," he said to my seven-year old daughter yesterday.

I can't fight his fist. His only power is hate, he fills himself by strangling me. It gives him relief. I watch the anger dissipate from his eyes, turning them black, as his shoulders relax, I see that strangling me is meditative for him. I choke and spit out something hard, white, and spit-laden. A tooth. My molar, at least nothing too obvious for anyone to see.

Monday, April 20

I've thought about killing him. Right there in front of the kids. I have the knife in my hand. But that would leave the children with no one. That's what's stopping me. I dig the knife into my palm instead and watch it cry blood.

Thursday, April 23

I can't live like this anymore. I think the worst thing about this lockdown is poverty and abuse intermingling together like lovers over weeks-long dates, no one really having an idea how much we're suffering under these safety measures.

The raw seed of bitterness in his irises

The hard knuckle in my mouth

No room.

Four walls mark our home-prison from the sickness outside, incubates the sickness inside, its metastasizing wrath culls our voices. The neighbors must not hear. My skin is now accessible to attacks 24/7. Oxygen is starting to taste like his manufactured poison. Our lifelines heave and whittle down from his threats crushing the air out from our lungs, slowly killing future possibilities that our souls will ever birth, from my children's children to other generations.

Friday, April 24

How can I calm the storms in his mind, in his fist; when my presence, when his job loss triggers him into anxiety, into fear, into emasculating fury that fluctuates and dams us shut? When reports by the second aggravate him. Water cuts earning me a punch. Permit rejections having me by the neck. We are all scared but his fear is toxic and I'm afraid my children will die from his poison. Better I take the beating for my children. I know this now: he could flog me with the bones of our dead children. I want to kill him so badly that to stop myself I strangled myself in the pit latrine yesterday until the avidity of that desperation dissipated...for now.

Sunday, April 26

My permit was rejected again.

I snuck out to the nearby supermarket. I'm standing in the grocery's aisles, strangling breathless pennies for more days for less hunger for more hope, the fluorescent lights screaming blight into the tops of my shoulders. The children are driving him crazy, and he wants to dump them and he yelled at them this morning, "I'll throw you over the fucking fence if you don't shut up."

Wednesday, April 29

He burned through my mobile data so he could follow updates online. Reports: lockdown extended. I sit on my knees and cry. Will my breath ever be considered essential?

Thursday, April 30

This morning when he sneaks through the streets to see a mate of his who's illegally brewing alcohol, I teach my children how to escape, how to align the chair under the window, push it open and climb out, using each other as support to land on the other side without falling.

It takes twenty-three tries for them to do it successfully without any adult help. Five minutes twenty-eight seconds it takes for them to make it out. What if that's too long and he's strangled me to death under three minutes, then what? I tell them it's a game and they'll need to know how to get far from the bad guys like the ones from the cartoons. Their nearest ally would be our neighbor, but her husband is too close with mine and several others. The oldest is only seven and gives me that look like she understands what I'm avoiding bluntly telling them: if their father kills me, they are in danger. She changes from that day on, and almost gets a spanking from my boyfriend because she doesn't respond to his calls and just stares at him strangely.

That night I sit on the floor scraping the calluses from his foot, realizing my plan won't work as the youngest can't even walk or run that far. If I was alone that'd be fine, but my children...

Sunday, May 3

We've been in lockdown for how long I can't even remember. A colleague who cleans with me at work is bored stiff from being at home all day. She used back roads where there are no police roadblocks to come to my house.

We sit behind the house by the tree where my boyfriend can't fully see our gestures and mannerisms. She pretends to not see the bruises on my face, neck and arms. Shows me the broadcast on her cellphone: "A startup AI-and-neuroscience-based anti-GBV NGO seeks beta testers for protective technology: 25–44-year-old people required, room & house boarding available (incl. dependents if you have), a monthly stipend. Review process less than 8 hours; unfortunately, marital approval required though a forfeit of certain rights will be accepted to work around it. Identities are kept confidential; no discrimination against sex, gender identity, sexual orientation, religious background, citizenship status, disability..."

I stop reading and hold the phone to my chest. Is this really happening? Am I going to be finally free and safe and financially independent? Will I now be able to take care of my kids without depending on him? My breaths flutter inside my chest like birds of hope, relief bubbles breaking the deadweight that holds their wings down. My children will be safe—their future will be safe. For the first time in my life I feel blessed to not be married and need the approval of a husband—that is freedom, and hell will no longer have us as its natives.

Monday, May 4

Another permit rejection just delivered this morning. I'm risking it: 17 hours from when I applied online through my friend's phone yesterday, notification received by word-of-mouth, friend of my friend. My reason to leave the house: to purchase medication prescribed by the gynecologist. As if I have one. Risking it. I'm leaving my children behind, certain that the friend of my friend is keeping watch from her house should anything suspicious occur in our home.

I wind through the graveled roads of our neighborhood, the back tarred road that connects to the parking lot of the supermarket. Walk behind to the empty delivery bay and stand by the black refuse skip. A door swings open and a slim figure surveys the area then walks to me. A store assistant, features concealed behind a mask.

"Dumelang," he whispers: hello, smiling. "I'm glad you could make it." From his pocket, he pulls out something wrapped in black plastic, then, checking the coast, whispers: "Listen, this from a start-up NGO advocating against GBV. Just report your findings to us for guaranteed payouts. Very confidential. Statistics so far are positive from people throughout the country. Not just women, but men also, people with disabilities—" He unwraps the black plastic, and several opalescent pills contained in a box sparkle in the daylight. "Make sure he consumes this. The tasing feature will electrocute him when he becomes physically or emotionally violent."

"How do I activate it?" I ask, hands trembling in the shadow of a high wall.

"Crush the pills and put it in his food. Works within minutes, a much quicker response than your crisis hotlines."

"Isn't that illegal?"

"Ain't it also illegal to physically harm someone? But that doesn't stop them, neither should this stop us."

"And then what happens?"

"Maybe he'll learn his lesson. But it sure as hell will stop him from kicking you if he's in pain."

My boyfriend's pain will speak louder than mine, which he'll listen to.

Something about my expression makes him say, "Don't worry. You're safe. You won't get caught. Even if his body was analyzed, it won't be detected in his system."

"All this sounds expensive...I don't have money on me." My jittery hands clasp the curls of my Afro.

"Sisi, pay us with your feedback and *we* pay you with financial rewards." I haven't felt kindness as sharp as this. "He tries to raise a hand at you, this stops him."

His hands wrap mine in these times when social distance is our salve, but it resolves my anxiety, this moment of stolen intimacy. My breath is essential, someone cares about it, and no I don't have to remain in hell anymore. Living in hell ends here in this space that my breath and my children's breath fill.

Finally, violence will taste like a summer song of a long-gone past and the souls of our breaths rise into the sky like a flock of birds migrating to new seasons of safety.

Interview with Tlotlo Tsamaase

INTERSTELLAR FLIGHT PRESS: What does the future mean to you?

TLOTLO TSAMAASE: It is unpredictable and sometimes scary. The only thing you can do is embrace every step you've taken forward and keep on moving.

IFP: How did you get your start writing?

TT: I was a very creative kid. I grew up building stuff with my hands, drawing a lot, and writing weird dialogues that my friends and I acted out. I fell in love with books and would spend my days and nights stuck in them, analyzing their words, and trying to extend their worlds with my own words, which was basically fan fiction. It felt quite empowering. Eventually, I started experimenting with my writing to create new worlds of my own.

IFP: What is your favorite thing about your own writing? Or about the process of writing?

TT: It's freeing. You're able to create your own universe and process emotions and problematic issues about the world, which is very therapeutic. Sometimes, you can create an identical world or quite an opposite one. It's all up to you, which is a very powerful act. The other part I love and sometimes find quite stressful is the research part of writing. You learn quite a lot of interesting things. The fun part is reading many other books and watching a lot of movies and tv series to refuel my creative juice, which gets quite depleted from overworking.

IFP: How does your identity/community/background influence your work?

TT: Every part of my identity influences the characters and the worlds that they come from. The way they speak. The way they dress. The texture of their hair. Most importantly the environment and society, which sometimes drives their choices.

IFP: How do you think we can build a better world as creatives?

TT: Creatives create worlds and refuges for readers. They show us different perspectives in quite an entertaining way. I believe the best thing is for a creative to never give up on their craft despite the obstacles. Before, readers from marginalized backgrounds never saw themselves depicted with nuance in film and books, and creatives allow us to see ourselves and understand different backgrounds. People find relief in books, films and any other creative project. To imagine a world without creative work would be so dull and sad. Of course, a better world is for every creative to receive access and publishing opportunities.

IFP: Let us know any upcoming projects or ways our community can support you:

TT: Well, my novella *The Silence of the Wilting Skin* (*Pink Narcissus Press*, 2020) is out now. It is about a nameless young woman living in the wards who slowly begins to lose her identity: her skin color is peeling off, people are becoming invisible, and the city plans to destroy the train where they bury their dead. You can find it where most books are published. Next year, I have a couple of projects coming out, particularly a horror story. Everyone can reach me on my website https://www.tlotlotsamaase.com/ and subscribe to my newsletter for updates on projects and possibly sneak-peaks, or potentially join my Patreon https://www.patreon.com/tlotlotsamaase. Also, just drop a "hello" or share any interests you have.

Leslie Archibald is a Houston based writer/reader, bending genre, and exploring multimedia literary projects. She is a graduate of the University of Houston and spends her spare time volunteering for Houston literary organizations and photographing her beautiful city. She is the winner of the 2017 *Spider Road Press* Spider's Web Flash Fiction contest. Her work appears in the special flash section of *Companion of the Ash* and *Tales of Texas Vol. 2*. She can be found at www.lesliearchibaldwriter.com, on Facebook at Leslie Mccoy Archibald, on Twitter @archardpress and Instagram @Leslie.Archibald.

Erin Becker writes middle grade, YA, essays, criticism, and poetry. Her work has appeared in *Barrelhouse Reviews, Lambda Literary,* and *Ms. Magazine,* among other outlets. She holds her MFA in Writing for Children and Young Adults from Vermont College of Fine Arts and her BA in English from the University of North Carolina at Chapel Hill, where she was a Morehead-Cain Scholar. Erin grew up in Cedar Rapids, Iowa. She lived in Patagonia for several years before moving to Washington, DC, where she runs a communications consultancy and writes The Storytelling Weekly newsletter. Erin's creative work is represented by Joanna Volpe at New Leaf Literary, and she's currently revising a middle grade novel. In her free time, you can find Erin hiking, running, and starting every sentence with "So I was listening to this podcast and..."

Cassandra Rose Clarke's work has placed in the Rhysling Awards and been nominated for the Philip K. Dick Award, the Romantic Times Reviewer's Choice Award, the Pushcart Prize, and YALSA's Best Fiction for Young Adults. She grew up in south Texas and currently lives in Houston, where she writes and serves as the executive director for Writespace, a literary arts nonprofit. She holds an M.A. in creative writing from The

University of Texas at Austin, and in 2010 she attended the Clarion West Writer's Workshop in Seattle. Her latest novel is *Forget This Ever Happened*, out now from *Holiday House*.

Raised in a suburb built over a swamp, **Laura Díaz de Arce** is a South Florida writer with a penchant for long-winded explanations and a nasty reading habit she can't seem to kick. Her other quirks include sudden exclamations in Spanish and talking to cats. Laura has a Master's in Literature, which is currently lost somewhere in her office closet. She is the author of *Monstrosity: Tales of Transformation* and *Mask of the Nobleman*. You can find her poorly spelled tweets and blurry photos on Twitter and Instagram @QuetaAuthor.

Nathan Elias grew up in Toledo, Ohio. He is the author of *The Reincarnations: Stories* and the forthcoming novel *Coil Quake Rift* (*Montag Press*, 2020/21). He holds an MFA in Creative Writing from Antioch University Los Angeles, his writing has been nominated for the Pushcart Prize and Best Microfiction, and he was a finalist of The Saturday Evening Post 2020 Great American Fiction Contest. His short fiction, poetry, essays, and book reviews have appeared in publications such as *PANK, Entropy, Hobart, Pithead Chapel*, and *Barnstorm*. He lives in Nashville, Tennessee with his wife and rescue dog.

Michael Glazner teaches high school English in the Houston area and spends his free time cleaning up after thunder-averse dogs.

Allison Hunt is an actor, writer, and teacher based out of New York City. She also co-wrote and stars in her own comedy series, Untitled Millennial Project. In her downtime, she loves reading dystopian and fantasy novels, learning about Astrology, and belting show tunes at the top of her lungs.

Nisola Jegede is the author of the short stories, Alungba and What Lies on the Other Side. A movie editor by day, writer by night, she received a bachelor degree in English and Literary Studies from Federal University, Oye-Ekiti. A Yoruba, she is a lover of movies, travelings and writer. She currently resides in a suburb part of Nigeria.

Jamileh Jemison (she/her) is an artist and scientist who has lived six lives of her own making (so far), and many hundreds more through reading. Inspired in early life by *Harriet the Spy, Sherluck Bones,* and *The Wind in* *the Willows*, observation, reinvention, ditching chores for adventure, and believing animals or plants might just talk to her are all active threads in her life. By day Jamileh shapes the development of digital health technology, by night she creates in many arenas of the arts. Her latest project is a Medusa musical in development. Find her on Twitter: @nuts2soup and on LinkedIn.

Justin C. Key is a speculative fiction writer and psychiatrist. His short stories have appeared in *The Magazine of Fantasy & Science Fiction, Strange Horizons,* and *Tor.com.* He is currently working on a near-future novel inspired by his medical training. When Justin isn't writing, working in the hospital, or exploring Los Angeles with his wife, he's trying to keep up with his three kids. You can follow his journey at justinckey.com and @JustinKey_MD on Twitter.

Annika Barranti Klein lives and writes in a tiny apartment in Los Angeles filled with books, bones, and unfinished knitting projects. Her fiction has been or is forthcoming in *Craft Literary, Hobart After Dark, Milk Candy Review, Mermaids Monthly,* and *Asimov's Science Fiction.* Her nonfiction is scattered throughout a multiverse of defunct websites. She is a copy editor by day and typically falls asleep watching television by night.

Andrea Kriz writes from Cambridge, MA. Her other stories have appeared in *Clarkesworld* and *Lightspeed,* among others. Find her at www.andreakriz.wordpress.com or on Twitter @theworldshesaw.

vanessa maki is a writer/author, visual artist, freelancer & horror enthusiast. She lives on Vancouver Island and is second generation Canadian. She dabbles in many literary genres / art forms and has a knack for experimenting.

Natachi Mez (she/her) is a Nigerian American writer, performer, and rapper from the Sacramento area in California. Natachi is a two-time finalist at the College Union Poetry Slam Invitational (CUPSI), and has featured at the Nuyorican Poets Cafe, Oberlin College, as well as at venues in Accra, Copenhagen, and Istanbul.

Natachi facilitates dynamic experiences that deepen audience engagement and celebrate community voice. Natachi has worked with youth communities and people who are incarcerated to engage writing and rapping as tools of empowerment. She has facilitated writing and performance workshops at Tufts University, Rutgers University, Rikers Island, and more.

Natachi graduated from Columbia University with a BA in Computer Science, and is a Business Program Manager, focusing on community building, communications, diversity, and design. You can find Natachi's words featured or forthcoming in *Unplug Mag, Gumbo Magazine, Breadcrumbs Magazine, Write About Now,* or on Instagram @natachi.life."

Archita Mittra is a writer, editor and artist, with a fondness for dark and fantastical things. She completed her B.A (2018) and M.A (2020) in English Literature from Jadavpur University and a Diploma in Multimedia and Animation from St. Xavier's College (2016). Her work has been published in *Strange Horizons, Mithila Review, Anathema Magazine, Thought Catalog* and elsewhere. When she isn't writing speculative fiction or drawing fanart, she can be found playing indie games, making jewelry out of recycled materials, reading a dark fantasy novel, baking cakes, or deciding which new Tarot deck to buy. She lives in Kolkata (India) with her family and rabbits. You can check out her blog (https://architamittra.wordpress.com/) and say hi on Twitter/Instagram @architamittra.

JT Morse is an award-winning, multi-genre writer/poet with a focus on character-driven narratives and hybrid works. She likes to dig deep, find magic in the mundane, and pry open doors with her wordsmithing skills. Morse's work has been published by *Balance of Seven Press, Texas Living magazine, Paragraph Planet, Central Coast Poetry Show, Haiku Journal, Nightmare Press,* and *Art Houston Magazine.* She's a facilitator/instructor at Writespace Houston and is frequently a featured panelist/presenter at literary festivals and cons across the U.S. Most of Morse's work is penned from her garden balcony at her mystical ranch in the Piney Woods of Texas, where she lives with her husband, daughter, and twenty-three spoiled-rotten rescue animals. Her website is perpetually in a state of flux, but you may be able to find out more about her at www.jtmorsewriter.com if you're lucky.

B. Narr is a writer and voice actor from Oklahoma. They write queer horror, wax poetic about monsters, and pretend to be other people. You can find their writing in publications like *Interstellar Flight Press, Nightmare Magazine,* and on Amazon. You can find their voice work in audio dramas like *The Silt Verses, The Waystation,* and *Retribution.* You can keep up with them on social media @sassylich, and on their website bnarr.com.

Sydney Richardson: A fairly average person through and through, Sydney is a born and raised Jersey girl with a Bachelor's in Liberal Studies from Syracuse University. Unable to settle in one place, she's constantly changing cities, but the one constant has been her lifelong love of speculative fiction. You can find some of Sydney's work at *Anathema Magazine,* and the Decoded 2020 Pride Anthology, and you can probably find her reading the poetic works of Nikki Giovanni.

Karen A. Romanko writes books about women and television. Her latest is *Women of Science Fiction and Fantasy Television* (McFarland, 2019), a follow-up to *Television's Female Spies and Crimefighters* (McFarland, 2016). She loves retro TV and discusses it on her blog Small Screen Pop. Karen lives in Los Angeles, where she enjoys walks on the beach and amateur photography.

Christina Sng is the two-time Bram Stoker Award-winning author of *A Collection of Dreamscapes* and *A Collection of Nightmares,* and Stoker-nominated essay *Final Girl: A Life in Horror.* Her poetry, fiction, essays, and art appear in numerous venues worldwide and have garnered many accolades, including the Jane Reichhold International Prize, nominations for the Rhysling Awards, the Dwarf Stars, the Pushcart Prize, as well as honorable mentions in the Year's Best Fantasy and Horror, and the Best Horror of the Year. Christina's next collection *The Gravity of Existence* is forthcoming in 2022. She lives in Singapore with her children and a menagerie of curious pets.

Bonnie Jo Stufflebeam's fiction and poetry has appeared in over 90 publications such as *Year's Best Dark Fantasy & Horror, Lightspeed,* and *LeVar Burton Reads,* as well as in six languages. By night, she has been a finalist for the Nebula Award. By day, she works as a Narrative Designer writing romance games for the mobile app Chapters. She lives in Texas with her partner and a mysterious number of cats.

Suhaila Sundararajan can usually be found holding a book, a teacher's manual, or a barbell, and she is forever running low on kids' bandaids. She currently writes on Medium about her life, including her experiences being a Muslim homeschooler on the spectrum with ADHD.

Kyle Tam is an author, dreamer, and full-time complainer. Her writing has previously been published in *EX/POST*, *Certified Forgotten*, and *Anime Feminist* among others. You can find her on Twitter at @PercyPropa, or at her website whatkylewrites.carrd.co.

Presley Thomas is a writer and teacher in Houston, TX. His work has appeared in *Interstellar Flight Press* and *New Body*.

Tlotlo Tsamaase is a Motswana writer of fiction, poetry, and architectural articles. Her work has appeared in *The Best of World SF Volume 1*, *Futuri uniti d'Africa*, *Clarkesworld*, *Terraform*, *Strange Horizons*, *Africanfuturism Anthology* and other publications. Her novella, *The Silence of the Wilting Skin*, is a 2021 finalist for the Lambda Literary Award. Her short story, *Behind Our Irises*, was shortlisted for the 2021 Nommo Awards. You can find her on Twitter and Instagram at @tlotlotsamaase and at www. tlotlotsamaase.com

John Tuttle is a Catholic man with a passion for truth and beauty. His writing has been published by *The Hill*, *Tablet Magazine*, *The Millions*, *Real Clear Science*, *Open Road Media*, *Voyage Comics & Publishing*, *An Unexpected Journal*, *University Bookman*, *Prehistoric Times Magazine*, and the University of Notre Dame's Grotto Network. His photography has appeared in several arts journals online and in print. He can be reached at jptuttleb9@gmail.com.

T.D. Walker is the author of the poetry collections *Maps of a Hollowed World* (*Another New Calligraphy* 2020) and *Small Waiting Objects* (*CW Books* 2019). Her science fiction poems and stories have appeared in *Strange Horizons*, *Web Conjunctions*, *The Cascadia Subduction Zone*, *Luna Station Quarterly*, and elsewhere. She curates Short Waves / Short Poems. Find out more at tdwalker.net.

Holly Lyn Walrath's poetry and short fiction has appeared in *Strange Horizons*, *Fireside Fiction*, *Daily Science Fiction*, *Luna Station Quarterly*, *Liminality*, and elsewhere. She is the author of the chapbooks *Glimmerglass Girl* (*Finishing Line Press*, 2018), *Numinose Lapidi* (in Italian, *Kipple Press*, 2020), and *The Smallest of Bones* (*Clash Books*, 2021). She holds a B.A. in English from The University of Texas and a Master's in Creative Writing from the University of Denver.

Corey J. White is the author of *Repo Virtual* and *The VoidWitch Saga - Killing Gravity, Void Black Shadow,* and *Static Ruin* - published by Tor.com Publishing. They studied writing at Griffith University on the Gold Coast, and are now based in Melbourne, Australia. Can be found on twitter at @cjwhite.

Interstellar Flight Press

Interstellar Flight Press is an indie speculative publishing house. We feature innovative works from the best new writers in science fiction and fantasy. In the words of Ursula K. Le Guin, we need "writers who can see alternatives to how we live now, can see through our fear-stricken society and its obsessive technologies to other ways of being, and even imagine real grounds for hope."

Find us online at www.interstellarflightpress.com.

 facebook.com/InterstellarFlightPress

 twitter.com/IntFlightPress

 instagram.com/InterstellarFlightPress

 patreon.com/InterstellarFlightPress

Amelia Gorman's *Field Guide to Invasive Species of Minnesota* is a poetic journey into the strange and wonderful world known previously only to the wild. Take a walk through the woods of Minnesota, past the Salton Sea, into the high grass of the prairie, beyond the rivers and creekbeds, into a world of the near-future where nature rules all. After all, the biggest ecological danger of invasive species is the monoculture they create.

Twelve by Andrea Blythe is a poetic retelling of the Brothers Grimm fairytale "The Twelve Dancing Princesses." Bewitching and beguiling, this short series of linked poems takes the reader to the underground realm and back, following the stories of twelve princesses and their life after the magic shoes.

Cthulhu meets hip-hop in this book of horror poems that flips the eldritch genre upside down. Lovecraftian-inspired nightmares are reversed as O'Brien asks readers to see Blackness as radically significant. *Can You Sign My Tentacle?* explores the monsters we know and the ones that hide behind racism, sexism, and violence, resulting in poems that are both comic and cosmic.